Not
Before
Sundown

Johanna Sinisalo

Not
Before
Sundown

Translated from the Finnish by
Herbert Lomas

Peter Owen
London and Chester Springs

PETER OWEN PUBLISHERS
73 Kenway Road, London SW5 0RE

Peter Owen books are distributed in the USA by
Dufour Editions Inc., Chester Springs, PA 19425-0007

English language edition first published in Great Britain
2003 by Peter Owen Publishers

Translated from the Finnish *Ennen Päivänlaskua Ei Voi*
© Johanna Sinisalo 2000
English translation © Herbert Lomas 2003

All Rights Reserved.
No part of this publication may be reproduced
in any form or by any means without the
written permission of the publishers.

ISBN 0 7206 1171 7

A catalogue record for this book is available from
the British Library

Printed and bound in Croatia
by Zrinski SA

For Hannu, Markku, Petri and Toni, who were there

The publishers thank the
Finnish Literature Information Centre
for providing a grant for the translation of this book.

Published with the assistance of Arts Council England

Part 1

Dusk Crept Through the Greenwood

Angel

I'm starting to get worried. Martes' face seems to be sort of fluctuating in the light mist induced by my four pints of Guinness. His hand's resting on the table close to mine. I can see the dark hairs on the back of his hand, his sexy, bony finger-joints and his slightly distended veins. My hand slides towards his and, as if our hands are somehow joined together under the table, his moves away in a flash. Like a crab into its hole.

I look him in the eyes. His face wears a friendly, open and understanding smile. He seems at once infinitely lovable and completely unknown. His eyes are computer icons, expressionless diagrams, with infinite wonders behind them, but only for the elect, those able to log on.

'So why did you ask me out for a drink? What did you have in mind?'

Martes leans back in his chair. So relaxed. So carefree.

'Some good conversation.'

'Nothing more?'

He looks at me as if I've exposed something new about myself, something disturbing but paltry: a trifle compromising, but not something that will inexorably affect a good working relationship. It's more as if my deodorant were inadequate.

'I have to tell you honestly that I'm not up for it.'

My heart starts pounding and my tongue responds on reflex, acting faster than my brain.

'It was you who began it.'

When we were little, having a bust-up in the schoolyard and looking for whose fault it was, that was the most important thing. Who began it.

And as I go on Martes looks at me as if I weren't responsible for my behaviour.

'I'd never have let myself in for this . . . if you hadn't shown me, so clearly, you *were* up for it. As I've told you, I'm shit hot at avoiding emotional pitfalls. If I've really no good reason to think the other person's interested I don't let anything happen. Not a thing. Hell, I don't even think it.'

Memories are crowding through my mind while I'm sounding off – too angrily, I know. I'm recalling the feel of Martes in my arms, his erection through the cloth of his trousers as we leaned on the Tammerkoski River railings that dark night. I can still feel his mouth on mine, tasting of cigarettes and Guinness, his moustache roughing my upper lip, and it makes my head start to reel.

Martes reaches for his cigarettes, takes one, flicks it into his mouth, flashes a light from his Zippo and inhales deeply, with deep enjoyment.

'I can't help it if I'm the sort of person people project their own dreams and wishes on to.'

In his opinion nothing has happened.

In his opinion it's all in my imagination.

I crawl home at midnight, staggering and limping – it's both the beer and the wound deep inside me. Tipsily, I'm licking my wound like a cat: my thought probes it like a loose tooth, inviting the dull sweet pain over and over again – dreams and wishes that won't stand the light of day.

The street lamps sway in the wind. As I turn in through the gateway from Pyynikki Square, sleet and crushed lime leaves blow in with me. There's loud talk in the corner of the yard.

A loathsome bunch of yobs are up to something in the corner by the rubbish-bins – young oafs, jeans hanging off their arses and their tatty windjammers have lifted to show bare skin. They've got their backs to me, and one of them's goading another, using that tone they have when they're challenging someone to perform some deed of daring. This time it's to do with something I can't see at their feet. Normally I'd give thugs like these a wide berth – they make my flesh creep. They're just the sort of slobs that make me hunch up my shoulders if I pass them in the street, knowing I can expect some foul-mouthed personal insult hurled at me – but just now, because of Martes, because I don't give a damn about anything and with my blood-alcohol count up, I go up to them.

'This is a private yard, it belongs to the flats. Trespassers will be prosecuted.'

A few heads turn – they sneer – and then their attention goes back to whatever's at their feet.

'Afraid it'll bite?' one asks another. 'Give it a kick.'

'Didn't you hear? It's a private yard. Now piss off.' My voice rises, my eyes sting with fury. An image from my childhood is flashing through my brain: a gang of bullies from an older class are towering above me, sneering at me, and goading me in that same tone – 'Afraid it'll bite?' – and then they stuff my mouth with gravelly snow.

'Stick it up your arse, sweetie,' one of these juvenile delinquents coos tenderly. He knows I've no more power over them than a fly.

'I'll ring the police.'

'I've rung already,' says a voice behind me. The tough old pensioner who lives on the floor below me and covers her rent by acting as some kind of caretaker has materialized behind me. The yobbos shrug their shoulders, twitch their leather jackets, blow their noses on to the ground with a swagger and dawdle away, as if of their own free will. They shamble off through the gateway, manfully swearing, and the last one flicks his burning fag-end at us like a jet-propelled missile. The slobs have hardly reached the street before we hear anxious running feet.

The lady snorts. 'Well, they did do what they were told.'

'Are the police coming?'

''Course not. Why bother the police with scum like that? I was off to the Grill House myself.'

The adrenaline's cleared my head for a moment, but now, as I struggle to dig out my keys, my fingers feel like a bunch of sausages. The woman's on her way to the gate, and that's fine, because my pissed brain's buzzing with a rigid, obsessive curiosity. I wait until she's off and start peering among the dustbins.

And there, tucked among the bins, some young person is sleeping on the asphalt in the yard. In the dark I can only make out a black shape among the shadows.

I creep closer and reach out my hand. The figure clearly hears me coming. He weakly raises his head from the crouching position for a moment, opens his eyes, and I can finally discern what's there.

It's the most beautiful thing I've ever seen.

I know straight away that I want it.

It's small, slender and it's curled up in a strange position, as if it were completely without joints. Its head is between its knees, and its full black mane of hair is brushing the muddy asphalt.

It can't be more than a year old. A year and a half at the most. A mere cub. By no means the huge bulk you see in illustrations of the full-grown specimens.

It's hurt or been abandoned, or else it's strayed away from the others. How has it got into the yard in the middle of the town? Suddenly my heart starts thumping and I swing around, half expecting to see a large black hunched shadow slipping from the dustbins to the gate and then off into the shelter of the park.

I react instinctively. I crouch down by it and carefully bend one of its forearms behind its back. It stirs but doesn't struggle. Just in case, I twist the strap of my bag all around the troll so that its paws are fastened tightly to its side. I glance behind me and lift it up in my arms. It's light, bird-boned, weighing far less than a child the same size. I glance quickly at the windows. There's nothing but a reddish light glowing in the downstairs neighbour's bedroom. The glamorous head of a young woman pops up in the window, her hand drawing the curtain. Now.

In a moment we're in my flat.

It's very weak. When I lower it on to the bed it doesn't struggle at all, just contemplates me with its reddish-orange feline eyes with vertical irises. The ridge of its nose protrudes rather more than a cat's, and its nostrils are large and expressive. The mouth is in no way like the split muzzle of a cat or a dog: it's a narrow, horizontal slit. The whole face is so human-looking – like the face of the American woolly monkey or some other flat-faced primate. It's easy to understand why these black creatures have always been regarded as some sort of forest people who live in caves and holes, beings accidentally created by nature as parodies of mankind.

In the light, its cubbishness is even more obvious. Its face and body are soft and round, and it has the endearing ungainliness of all young animals. I examine its front paws: they're like a rat's or racoon's, with flexible, jointed fingers and long nails. I remove my bag strap from around it, and the cub makes no move to scratch or bite. It just turns on its side and curls up, drawing its tufted tail between its thighs and folding its front paws against its chest. Its tangled black mane falls over its nose, and it lets out that half-moan/half-sigh of a dog falling asleep.

I stand at the bedside, looking at the troll-cub and taking in a strong smell – not unpleasant, though. It's like crushed juniper berries with a hint of something else – musk, patchouli? The troll hasn't moved an inch. Its bony side heaves to the fast pace of its breathing.

Hesitantly I take a woollen blanket from the sofa, stand by the bed a while and then spread it over the troll. One of its hind legs gives a kick, like a reflex, swift and strong as lightning, and the blanket flies straight over my face. I struggle with it, my heart pumping wildly, for I'm convinced the frightened beast will go for me, scratching and biting. But no. The troll still lies there curled up and breathing peacefully. It's only now that I face the fact that I've brought a wild beast into my home.

My head and neck are aching. I've been sleeping on the sofa. It's ridiculously early; still dark. And there's nothing on the bed. So that's what it's all been: a fantasy that won't survive the first light of day.

Except that the blanket lies crumpled on the floor by the bed, and there's a faint little sound coming from the bathroom.

I get up and walk slowly, in the light of the streetlamps filtering through the window, creeping as quietly as I can to the bathroom door. In the dusk I can see a small bony black bottom, hind legs, a tufted twitching tail, and I realize what's happening. It's drinking from the lavatory bowl. The juniper-berry smell is pungent. Then I spot a yellow puddle on my mint-green tiled floor. Naturally.

It has stopped lapping up water and has sensed that I'm there. Its torso is up from the bowl so fast I can't see the movement. Its face is dripping with water. I'm trying to convince myself that the water is perfectly clean, drinkable. I'm trying to remember when I last twirled the brush around the bowl and put lavatory cleaner in. Its eyes are still dull, it doesn't look healthy, and its pitch-black coat is sadly short of gloss. I move aside from the bathroom door, and it slides past me into the living-room, exactly as an animal does when it's got another route to take – pretending to be unconcerned but vividly alert. It walks on two legs, with a soft and supple lope: not like a human being, slightly bent forwards, its front paws stretched away from its sides – ah, on tiptoe, like a ballet dancer. I follow it and watch it bounce on to my bed, effortlessly, like a cat, as though gravity didn't exist – then curl up and go back to sleep again.

I go back to the kitchen for a cereal bowl, fill it with water and put it by the bed. Then I start mopping up the bathroom floor, though I've got a splitting headache. What the hell do trolls eat?

Back in my study, I leave the door open, boot up my computer, connect to Navigator and tap out the word TROLL.

http://www.finnishnature.fi

Troll (older forms: hobgoblin, bugbear, ogre), *Felipithecus trollius*.
Family: Cat-apes (Felipithecidae)
    A pan-Scandinavian carnivore, found only north of the Baltic and
in Western Russia. Disappeared completely from Central Europe along
with deforestation but, according to folklore and historical sources, still
fairly common in medieval times. Officially discovered, and scientifically
classified as a mammal, as late as 1907. Before that assumed to be a
mythical creature of folklore and fairy tale.
    Weight of a full-grown male: 50–75 kg. Height standing upright:
170–190 cm. A long-limbed plantigrade, whose movements nevertheless show digitigrade features. Walk: upright on two legs. Four long-
nailed toes on the hindlimbs, five on the forelimbs, both including a
thumb-like gripping toe. The tail long, with a tuft. The tongue rough.
The overall colour a deep black, the coat dense, sleek. A thick black
mane on the head of the males. Movement only at night. Main nourishment: small game, carrion, birds' nests and chicks. Hibernates. Cubs
probably conceived in the autumn before hibernation, the female giving
birth to one or two cubs in spring or early summer. About the behaviour
of this animal, however, so extremely shy of human contact, there is
very little scientific knowledge. Extremely rare. Supposedly there are
about four hundred specimens in Finland. Classified as an endangered
species.

Angel

This is making me no wiser. I click on SEARCH and come up with the following:

http://www.netzoo.fi/mammals/carnivores

Because of their great outward resemblance to humans or apes, trolls were originally mistaken for close relatives of the hominids; but further study has demonstrated that the case is one of *convergent evolution*. Considered a primate, the species was first erroneously designated 'the Northern Troglodyte Ape' – Latin *Troglodytas borealis*. Later it was observed that the troll belonged to a completely independent family of carnivores the *Felipithecidae*, but the apelike attributions survived for a time in the nomenclature, *Felipithecus troglodytas*. At present, the established, scientifically accepted nomenclature of the species still bows to popular tradition as *Felipithecus trollius*. An interesting episode in the naming of the troll was a suggestion from the prestigious *Societas pro Fauna et Flora*: relying on the mythical and demonic connotations, they proposed the name *Felipithecus satanus*.

Only one other species of the *Felipithecidae* is known, the almost extinct yellow cat-ape (*Felipithecus flavus*), a roughly lynx-sized creature whose habitat is the heart of the Indonesian rain forest. The common ancestor of the species is believed, on fossil evidence, to have inhabited South-East Asia.

Though, on the evidence of its mode of life and dentation, the troll is clearly a carnivore, many scientists consider that the species does not properly belong to the order of *Carnivora*. Theories exist that the troll is more closely related to the insectivores and primates than to the true feline predators, and this is supported by certain anatomical features.

It has been suggested that several other species whose existence has not been scientifically established beyond doubt (such as the legendary Tibetan 'Abominable Snowman', or Yeti, of hearsay, and the mythical North American Sasquatch, or 'Big Foot') may also be humanity-shunning representatives of the *Felipithecidae* family.

Firm proof of the existence of *Felipithecus trollius* was not obtained until 1907, when the Biological and Botanical Department of the Tsar Alexander University of Helsinki received the carcass of a full-grown troll that had been discovered dead. There had been previous reports of first-hand sightings of trolls, but this legendary creature, oft-mentioned in folk tradition and in the *Kalevala,* was considered a purely mythical beast in scientific circles. Clearly, the occasional troll-cub encountered in the wilderness served to maintain myths of gnomes and goblins, especially since there is a theory that the trolls regulate any great increase in their population by abandoning new-born offspring.

The troll's ability to merge with the terrain, the inaccessibility of its habitat, its shyness of human contact, its silent night-habits and its hibernation in cave-dens, causing them rarely to leave snow tracks, may partially explain the late discovery of the species. The troll's zoological history is thus very similar to those of, for example, the okapi, not identified until 1900, the Komodo dragon (1912) and the giant panda (1937). In spite of abundant oral tradition and many sightings by the aboriginal population, these animals were long classified by scientists as myth and folklore. It is worth remembering that an estimated 14 million subspecies of animals live on the planet, of which only about 1.7 million are recognized and classified, or less than 15%. The relatively large cloven-footed animals, *Meganuntiacus vuquangensis* and *Pseudoryx nghetinhensis*, for example, were discovered as late as 1994 . . .

Angel

As I sit at my computer I glance from time to time at the bedroom. When I was drunk it seemed such a hell of a good idea to bring this touching, rejected wild-animal cub into my pad. An animal that may grow as much as two metres tall.

But even now, when I'm totally sober, the animal has something absolutely captivating about it. Is it just its visual grace to a professional's eye?

Or is it that as soon as I see something beautiful I have to possess it? With my camera or with my eye or with my hand? With the shutter or by shutting the door?

Even though I won't know what to do with it?

But nothing changes the fact that the creature's still small. And sick. And weak. And totally abandoned.

I print off a whole load of internet material, without feeling it's any help. I return to netzoo and click on EVOLUTION.

I learn that 'convergent evolution' refers to species that develop in ways resembling each other without there being any close zoological relationship. Good examples are the shark, the ichthyosaur and the dolphin, which have developed from completely different vertebrate forms: the shark from fish, the ichthyosaur from land-dwelling reptiles and the dolphin from land mammals. Nevertheless, they've all developed into streamlined, finned and tailed animals in the same ecological group: swift piscivorous marine predators. There are many other examples: grassland-dwelling flightless birds, such as the emu, the ostrich and the extinct moa; or such semi-aquatic marine creatures as seals, sea-lions and herbivorous sirenians, notably the dugong and the endangered manatee.

I'm becoming hellishly well informed. According to the entry, convergent evolution means that, in widely separated terrains, the same atmospheric and environmental conditions can, through their physical properties, produce similar kinds of living organisms from totally different prototypes. Cases of convergent evolution are, on the one hand, the trolls and the South-East Asian cat-apes, derived from a small arboreal animal slightly resembling the mustelid or racoon, and, on the other, the apes and hominids derived from proto-primate mammals. Both occupied the same ecological niche, where bipedalism and prehensile forefingers were survival factors for the species . . .

Nothing to help me, though.

I look at my machine. It's just a machine.

I'll have to try elsewhere.

I can only speculate about the effect of the telephone beeping at Dr Spiderman's – at my old flame Jori Hämäläinen's, that is – 'Hämä-hämä-hämäläinen', because getting worked up always makes him stammer. Hämähäkki being Finnish for spider, he's naturally been dubbed 'Spiderman'. Eight beeps go before he replies, and his voice reveals he's ready to flip his lid.

First I fumble for the customary 'How are things?', etc., but I know that this road will soon be blocked.

'Sweet Angel, golden-haired cherub,' comes Spider's slightly nasal, taunting voice. 'It's not very long ago you gave me a very nasty kick in the gluteus – after scarcely a couple of months of your angelic blessings. So what, I wonder, makes you call me up now. And especially at this early hour.'

I splutter something about how I thought we'd agreed to be friends.

'I was beginning to think your mother had talked you round – she always did dream you'd be partners with a real doctor, didn't she?' Spider lashes out, making me blush. Then his tone changes, sounding almost interested. 'You didn't manage to net that guy, did you?'

It's already coming home to me that this call is a terrible mistake, but Spiderman goes on relentlessly.

'There you were, your great blue eyes moist with tears, trying to stammer out that I'm not your type, that I'm not the right one, and how "you'd be wounding me if you went on with a relationship where you yourself couldn't be a hundred per cent committed". And meanwhile you were going on about that other guy the whole time.'

Was I really? Hell, it was possible. As if I could have possessed him by talking about him, throwing his name about, would-be casually.

'You really relished his name on your tongue. Martti, Martti – Martti this and Martti that. Guess how flagrant and repellent it sounded. And it was crystal clear that all your would-be serious, pretty little speech meant was this: you wanted me out of the way, so you could be free to step on the gas when this object of distant adoration – obviously your right-and-proper future commitment – gave the green light. Or what?'

I'm speechless. Incapable of anything else.

'So then. What do you want?'

I clear my throat. This isn't going to be easy.

'What do you know about trolls?'

There's a howl of satanic laughter in my ear. 'Angel, darling, now I must have your permission to be inquisitive. Are you writing an essay for school?'

I mumble something stupid about having a bet on it. 'You know,' I wind up helplessly, 'about the sorts of things they eat.' I can feel the receiver radiating embarrassed silence into Spiderman's ear.

He finally bursts out, 'You ring an expensive veterinary surgeon at eight-thirty on a Sunday morning to ask *what trolls eat?*'

I know Spider can be a devil and always is, given the chance, but then he's never been able to resist an opportunity to show off his knowledge either. I'm right. A familiar lecturing tone creeps into his voice.

He starts ticking items off. 'Frogs, small mammals. They rob birds' nests. Sometimes they've been reported as preying on lambs in outlying fields, but that's probably just rumour. There's a theory that they fish with their paws, like bears, which I've no reason to doubt. Hares. Game birds. Now and then a reindeer-calf caught by the leg can end up as a troll's dinner. Sometimes they harass white-tailed deer, too. They eat carrion when they come across it. A full-grown individual requires a kilo or two of animal protein a day. Any more questions?'

I nod at the receiver and let out assenting noises.

'Definitely carnivores, but not omnivorous like, for instance, bears. Similar digestive system to cats. So if you're punting on the troll's diet as gnawing at spruce shoots by moonlight, your money's down the drain. And if you want more information, Angel, my fairy queen, go to the library and consult Pulliainen's *The Large Predators of Finland*.'

And then, cuttingly, he hangs up on me.

Iivar Kemppinen, *Finnish Mythology*, 1960

As with the folklore of other peoples, Finnish mythology finds a significant place for not only ghosts and fairies but many demonized animals, particularly the bear, the troll, the wolf, the snake, the lizard, the frog, the weasel, the shrew, the wasp, the death-watch beetle and the louse. Demonic animals differ from ghosts and fairies in that they are usually clearly visible and recognizable, with the exceptions of the shy and secretive troll and the weasel. Sometimes, however, a demonic creature is so closely identified with faerie existence that a creature – the troll, for example – may be offered sacrificial food on an altar stone; and a pet snake has been accused of being a witch's 'familiar spirit' (*Finnish Folklore Archives*, Karttula, Juho Oksanen, No. 10129; Sortavala, Matti Moilanen, No. 2625).

Demonic animals have been much discussed in international scientific literature, and various theories have been presented. Finnish folklore itself has its own explanation for the demonic resonance and significance of the above animals: they are predatory or otherwise baneful beasts generated by Pohjola or Manala, the Underworld or Hades of northern Finnish folklore, and sent to be a torment and a scourge on the face of the earth. As representatives of the malign powers of Manala they are hated but at the same time propitiated and placated. Thus, if anyone does harm to these semi-supernatural creatures, such as a pet snake or frog, they will bring misfortune on themselves.

Tapio, the tutelary genius of the forest, originally personified the forest, the spirit of the forest, and as such is one of the earth sprites (Ganander, 1.89; Gottlund, 1.350). The genius of the gloomy forests is also called Hiisi, or Demon. Thus Tapiola and Hiitola, as names for the forest, mean they are the dwelling places of Tapio or Hiisi. But sometimes the forest itself is given the appellation Tapio or Hiisi, without any reference to a guardian or the forest fauna (SKVR VII 1, No. 810, 823). Similarly the Karelians refer to the forest people as Hiisi's people, and Hiisi has acquired a Demon's reputation as a representative of the malign forces of Manala. In the parish of Hiitola the forestlands are called Hiisi's hills (*Hiijje miät* in the Karelian dialect), where bad Hiisis, or Demons, are said to live. Also, in a Karelian dialect, *metšh* (Finnish *metsä,* forest) means 'the devil' (Kujola, 1.234–35). This identification of the forest people with the Underworld's people, the Demon's people, has clearly occurred because the dark forest, with its bears, wolves, trolls and other bugbears, was frightening, so that it was an easy transition to equate it with Manala, the fabled breeding place of the beasts of prey, given birth to by the Mistress of Pohjola, the Northland (§313).

Angel

On the bed a lustreless black flank is heaving feverishly. Wild-cat digestion.

I dash to the fridge and poke about frantically. Orange marmalade, kalamata olives, fresh but already somewhat wilted chilli, Bavarian Blue cheese.

A cat. A cat. What do cats eat?

Catfood.

And in a flash I recollect something: what's the guy's name downstairs? Kaikkonen? Korhonen? Koistinen? The man with the young foreign wife. They've got some sort of a pet. Once I saw the man opening the front door, about to go in, and he was carrying a red-leather harness.

So they've got a cat, for I've seen neither of them walking a dog.

Palomita

Sleep's a well – I float up from it like a bubble. The water's black honey. My arms and legs are trying to stir in the syrupy night. I drag my lids open, so my eyes smart.

I'm damp with sweat and my heart's starting to race. For a moment I think the sound I hear is the bell on the bar counter back at Ermita. The bell that orders me out of the back room. But luckily my hand touches something, my eyes open, and I'm surrounded by the grey-blue of the room's make-believe night.

I've been in a very deep sleep, as I always am when Pentti's away. When I'm alone, as soon as I drop off I feel I'm spinning downwards. I don't need to tense every bit of my body, like when Pentti's beside me. No need to wake up at every sound. Pentti, when he's asleep, sounds like someone suffocating.

The ringing isn't at all like the horrible silvery bar-bell at Ermita. It's tinnier and rougher and makes you jump. Ring-ring-ring it goes in the empty hall that Pentti's removed all the coats from and locked them up in the closet for the time he's off on his trip. I slip my slippers on and get my bathrobe off the chair. The bell rings again and again, as if some-one's in a terrible state. I get the footstool out of the cupboard and climb on it to peep through the peephole.

It's the man from upstairs who's ringing the bell. He's fair and tall and curly-haired. I've seen him once before on the staircase out-side.

I've learned always to look through the peephole. Pentti doesn't want me to open the door to anyone except those he's told me to. The peephole's a well, where little crooked people live. Many times a day I get on to the stool and look out at the staircase. There aren't often people there, but whenever I see one it's a reward. The man rings the bell once more, and then he tosses his head. He's giving up.

I've no idea why I'm doing it. But cautiously I open the door.

He's speaking Finnish fast, and I can only pick up a word here and there. The words are twisty and misty, and they've long bits that ought to be said with your mouth open right to the back. Lucky for me I don't have to depend much on Finnish, as Pentti hardly says anything and I don't go anywhere.

The man says, 'Excuse me.' He says his name, which I can't hear properly, but it sounds like Miguel. He says he's from the floor above, and he keeps on asking for some sort of food and repeating some word I simply don't know.

It seems to be dawning on him that I don't understand. Up to now he's only been able to see his own problem, but now he's beginning to see me. He begins speaking English, which I understand better, though not very well anyway, because at home we spoke Chabacano and Tagalog in the village, and they had to cut school short for me.

'Catfood?' he asks. 'Have you any catfood you could lend me?'

In spite of myself, a smile crosses my face. We haven't got a cat. Pentti wouldn't put up with anything like that. Once, when he was drunk again, he took a lucky doll I'd been given by Conchita at the bar and flushed it down the lavatory. He'd noticed I used to nurse it in my arms sometimes, before going to bed. The doll blocked the drain, and Pentti had to pump away with a plunger for ages before it flushed clear again.

I shake my head and say no, no catfood. I ask if he speaks Spanish, but he signals no, with troubled eyes. I grope for some English words, trying to help. Just around the corner there's a big kiosk that sells almost everything. One evening Pentti sent me to get some beer there, gave me some money and a piece of paper with the order scribbled on. I handed them over to the kiosk-keeper, and he handed me back six cold brown bottles. I didn't know I was supposed to get a receipt, and when I got back Pentti said I'd kept some of the change. Myself, I did think they were a bit dear. I haven't been back to the kiosk since, but I do remember it was stocked with almost as much stuff as the market.

Miguel wrinkles his forehead. I feel sorry for him. I can't understand why he can't run those two blocks to this kiosk, which is almost a little department store, but I'm eager to think of some way to help him. I think about cats, I think about what they eat. Cats swarm in the harbour. They love fish.

I leave the door open and rush into the kitchen. I open the freezer and take out a packet from a big bag of packed coley Pentti bought on special offer. The packets rattle like firewood. I go back to the door and push a frosty packet into Miguel's hand.

'The microwave. Put it in the microwave,' I say, clearly. Those are words I've often heard, and I know them well. Miguel stares at the packet of fish and shifts it from hand to hand because it's so cold.

He squeezes the packet. Thanks flow from his lips in a mixture of English and Finnish. And then he's off, hopping up the stairs, a man with an angelically beautiful face and hair like a wheatfield in sunshine. I hear the door slam shut on the floor above.

Angel

I must try to pay this back in some way, I reflect, as I push the coley into the microwave. She must be a Filipino, for she speaks a little English and Spanish, but she looks so Asiatic. Is she more than sixteen years old? A bought bride, she must be, purchased for the old geezer down below at some marriage market.

And they have no cat. My face glows: I ought to have been quicker on the uptake about that pretty, soft, red-leather harness.

I switch the indicator to 'defrost' and switch the oven on. When the humming begins, the troll's ears prick up. It gives a jerk but, as nothing's threatening it, it calms down again. The smell of fish spreads through the room. I take the dish out of the microwave and test the fish with my finger. It's warm around the edges and has begun to turn pale; it's frozen in the middle, but most of it is at room temperature and a gelatinous grey. I slice some pieces off the defrosted bits, put them on aluminium foil and take them into the living-room. The troll's nostrils tremble, but it shows no interest in what it smells. I take some fish in my hand and sit on the edge of the bed. The troll opens its eyes slightly and regards me with its vertical pupils. I hold a piece of fish close to its nostrils, its mouth. It sniffs at the fish faintly, wearily, then closes its eyes again and turns its head away almost humanly. It curls its bony, slender black back towards me, and its belly gives out a very, very small but recognizable sound: the rumble of hunger.

Aki Bärman, *The Beast in Man: An Enquiry Concerning the Kinship Between Man and Wild Animal in Myth and Fantasy,* 1986

The transformation of a human being into an animal, or an otherwise close metamorphic kinship of human and animal, is an almost universal feature of world mythology, a mythical stratum evidently based on the 'animal roles' of shamanism and totemism. In general, the animal metamorphoses and animal kinships manifested in various cultures are connected to some fearful beast of prey endemic to the cultural area in question (in Asia the tiger, in South America the jaguar, in Europe the wolf and in Scandinavia the bear, as well as, and in particular, the troll). The essences of the human and the animal are intermingled, and a complex narrative tradition develops around the animal, involving – as in werewolf stories, for example – definite regularities, such as the effect of the full moon, the slaughter of the werewolf with a silver bullet, methods of becoming a werewolf and so on. In the case of Finland, perhaps a larger proportion of this type of recurrent narrative material is associated with the troll.

Owing to the pseudo-humanoid external characteristics of the troll, the Finnish narratives concerning its origins have acquired a Christian colouring. According to one version, the trolls came into being when Adam and Eve had given birth to so many children they began to feel shame about it, and they hid some of their children in caves, intending to keep them from God's notice. The children ended up by living so long beneath the ground they changed into trolls. Iceland harbours a similar story. Another Finnish version relates that the trolls were born during the Deluge. People were lazy and could not be bothered to follow Noah's example and build arks; instead they ascended the hills in order to escape the flood. The time spent in the caves brought its own punishment on their heads: when the waters abated, the people had turned into trolls. These narratives clearly indicate that trolls were considered representatives of a degenerate species of the human race. Similar conceptions pertain to, among other creatures, anthropoid apes in many primitive cultures.

According to the Scandinavian notions above, therefore, trolls were created by God and were indeed members of the divine creation – not supernatural beings – but in one way or another had acted against God's will. The priests tried to dismiss the pagan imagery associated with these creatures, but certain of the original beliefs survived even into the period when the trolls had been verified as an animal species like any other. An interesting feature of the topic is that, owing to the effect of Christian belief, many troll-narratives based on folk tradition have been transformed into tales about demons. In Finland, for instance, hundreds of narratives are recorded that show how cunning individuals discomfit and dupe simple-minded fiends – which, in the more venerable versions, are almost exclusively trolls. Thus, on the evidence of these narratives, our ancestors had a particular need to emphasize their own superiority and pre-eminence in comparison with this somewhat anthropomorphic animal.

The typical attributes of the mythical trolls were ugliness, hirsuteness and habitation inside mountains and rocks. They were agents of the dark powers, and they turned into stone in the light of day. Often the trolls were held to be servants of Satan, lying in wait for people at night and snatching them off to their caves. The phrase for these abductions was: 'They were carried off to the mountain.' The victims the trolls either killed or held as prisoners until insanity ensued.

Malign trolls of this sort also appear in the Scandinavian Viking tradition. Odin and his brothers killed the giant Ymir, after which the giant's rotting body began to be infested with maggots, both black and white. The gods called the maggots forth and gave them form and intelligence, and from the black maggots, which were by nature cunning and treacherous, the gods created the trolls; and since the trolls were in this manner born from the flesh of Ymir, out of which the earth was also created, the gods decided that the trolls should continue their existence as part of the earth and rock. In consequence, the trolls came to live beneath the earth, and in so far as they erred by penetrating up into the daylight they were punished for their crime with petrifaction, becoming rocks themselves. On the other hand, the poem 'The Seeress's Prophecy' in the poetic Edda states the lineage of the trolls to be that of the tribe of the wolf Fenrir. The trinity of the wolf, the troll and man is indeed a fascinating and illuminating aspect of the werewolf myth.

Finnish tradition also hands down stories of benign and harmless trolls who have lived with human beings on such good terms of mutual understanding that they have even married into named families. There are also numerous stories of girls having given birth to children sired by trolls and of youths seeking troll brides; and these are altogether in the class of the ancient myths about animal consorts.

Tales of trolls adopting human babies as their own cubs have been recorded all the way from China to North America and its Indian tribes. Though, as a species, the troll never spread beyond the Bering Strait, it is conceivable that ancestors of the Indians migrating to Alaska via the Chukotskiy peninsula may have transported this narrative tradition with them (cf. e.g. the Alaskan monster, the *alascattalo*, a hybrid of the moose and the walrus, whose name is etymologically reminiscent of the Lapland creature, the *staalo*, whose legend is clearly a variation of the troll legend). It can in fact be asserted that the troll has maintained a very special symbolic position among the northern peoples for thousands of years.

Angel

It looks at me like a puppy-dog, but there are live coals in its orange eyes.

It's lying curled up in a ball. I go to the bedside gingerly and hold my breath as I sit down on the edge of the bed beside it and observe its slender, heaving black sides, its helpless but sinewy being. Suddenly its paw straightens out. Its long supple fingers and fierce nails come towards me, and I almost snatch my hand away but don't, I don't, and its fingers wrap around my wrist for a moment; its hot slender paw touches me for a fleeting moment, and my eyes fill with tears.

Three days have gone by, and it simply isn't eating.

Ancient Poems of the Finnish People, II. 3. 3410, 1933
Village of Kitee: 'Repo-Matti Väkeväinen's Powerful Spell'

If the Lord willn't grant my will,
And lets me be alone,
Then grant me thou my will,
Old man behind the hill,
Old man beneath the stone!

Angel

Dr Spiderman had mentioned birds' nests. I tried a raw egg first, cracked into a bowl, then an unshelled one, but it wouldn't have either of them. I went to the supermarket for some quails' eggs, and it did show a little interest in these, but perhaps it was just their colour, spottedness and small size reminding it of something. Anyway it didn't eat those either.

I look at the black figure on the bed, at once restless, exhausted and – it's obvious – painfully hungry. I can't let it outside. Out there are the thugs in their steel-toe-capped boots, getting their thrills by drenching drunks with petrol, throwing cats from the roofs of multi-storey blocks and mugging gays. And if I tell anyone I'll just as certainly lose the creature.

Its juniper-berry smell plays in my nostrils. Its own species didn't want it. It was too much – ballast, a burden. They abandoned this light, slender, supple being, worthy of being immortalized in black marble.

Back to the cursed highway of knowledge, to the electronic asphalt, stretching in all directions, with no path leading where it should: to the forest.

For the hell of it, I put the cursor on to the *Kalevala* link of netzoo and click there. The *Kalevala* site has its own index. I wait briefly while the machine scrolls up references to trolls and demons. There's no end of them. The biggest group is in the poem called 'The Demon Skis', where Lemminkäinen, skiing along, is chasing a demon that's scampering away from him, and the demon, as it frisks off, sends the stewpots flying in a Lapland village. I log on to the bride's guide poem, 'Instructions and a Warning'. Here the bride complains about her bridegroom, and this makes me think of the Filipino girl downstairs:

> I'd be better off
> in better places,
> with larger lands,
> and roomier rooms,
> a fuller-blooded man,
> better built;

I'm given to this no-good,
left with this loafer:
took his carcass from a crow,
robbed his nose from a raven,
mouthed like a famished wolf,
haired like hell's troll,
bellied like a bear.

That's the complete demon reference. I wasn't expecting to find instructions for feeding trolls in the *Kalevala*, but, surprisingly, the falling metre sweeps you along. The following troll fragment is, very aptly, Väinämöinen's, which he sings to the accompaniment of a kantele.

None in the forest
that loped on four legs,
that bounded and bobbed,
but lingered to listen,
suck in some ecstasy:
squirrels came switching
from leaf-spray to leaf-spray,
stoats came and stopped there,
settled on fences.
Elks hopped on the heath,
lynxes leaped about laughing.
A wolf woke in the swamp,
a troll rose on the rocks,
a bear reared on the heath
from its pen in the pines,
its den in the spruce thicket.

I've had my fill of the *Kalevala*. The SEARCH function locates links here and there – to biology, mythology, various fairy tales and old stories in their hundreds if not thousands. But nothing concrete. I'll have to look elsewhere.

I've already been out of the flat several times, and every time I come back to find my troll in the same place on the bed, heart-rendingly in almost the same position, scarcely able to raise its head.

Yrjö Kokko, *Pessi And Illusia,* 1944

'What . . . ?' exclaimed the woodpecker, gazing down inquisitively. It saw something that looked like a span-sized human being, though the creature had thick brown fur and a squirrel's tufty ears, as well as a hare's funny little stumpy tail. It peeped up at the woodpecker with happy and friendly eyes. Actually, perhaps the eyes seemed too small, but that may have been because of the rather large nose, with an equally large mouth beneath it, broadening into a happy smile and revealing beautiful pearl-white rows of teeth. Also, the creature's hands and feet were perhaps on the large side, and its fur seemed matted, with longish hair dangling from the top of its head to its neck. Obviously, this was a small forest troll, waking up from its winter sleep – not a relative of those large black predatory animals that prowled the Lapland boulders in the summers, looking for prey, or at the most a second cousin twice removed – but a gnome, the little friendly creature found in fairy stories.

Angel

I lower the children's book I've been reading here in the library reading-room. From his description it's clear that Yrjö Kokko had never seen a photograph of a real troll. But the pile of books on my library table, which I've been scouring under the heading TROLL, show that it's no wonder: sightings of trolls were extremely rare, and photographs rarer still, until the 1970s, when automatic cameras, hides and weeks-long watches over carcasses became the fashion. Before that, trolls were never hunted: the flesh was uneatable, the carcass nauseatingly smelly. There was known to be some small market for trolls' winter coats: in a small way the Russians went in for trapping trolls in the autumn, but it was a rather unprofitable business. The trolls very rarely fell into traps, and it was almost impossible to hunt them down with guns, for they were silent and swift night-creatures. Hunting dogs were tried but with hopeless results: either the trolls put the dogs totally off the scent, or, if they were cornered, mauled the dogs with murderous fury. A dog with a bull-terrier type temperament, the *rollikoira* or troll-hound, much prized in Russia, does still exist. It's a variant of the Karelian bearhunter and is said to have more than a little strain of the wolf and the husky in it. But the troll-hound (its real name, I hear, is the Ladoga bloodhound) has not been used for hunting for a long time.

Also, it was no use looking for trolls, like bears, in their winter dens, for the cavities the troll seeks out for hibernation are so inaccessible that there was almost no point in looking for their breathing holes. And there was no reason to cull them to stop them competing with human hunters on game preserves, for in winter they were completely out of the running and in summertime they were more interested in lemmings than elks. For a few years a bounty was offered for killing them, because the Lapps wailed that the wolverines and *staalos* were rampaging among the reindeer herds, costing more than tax inspectors. But then the nature preservationists and animal-rights people intervened.

I dive even deeper into the lore. Certain Hanseatic traders were familiar with the term *Spukenfell* – literally 'spookskin' – which referred to a rare and expensive item, as mythical as mummified mermaids and unicorns. In Russia in the early twentieth century a few trolls were successfully caught in traps, and the thick silky-black spookskin flayed from a full-sized male in its winter coat was apparently an imposing sight. One Politburo official had a spookskin hanging over the fireplace in the guest-room of his dacha, with the head still attached. I'm revolted.

I again read Kokko's description of a troll. Leaving out the size, it's not so wide of the mark. The brown coat of fur, though, is actually pitch-black, the ears are not tufty at all, and the 'funny little stumpy tail' – oh, so cute – is a lashing, tuft-ended snake, a trembling mood-antenna. A rather large nose – hmmm – perhaps it will be later when the face elongates into more of a muzzle. The mouth is not particularly big either. When it 'draws back into a happy smile', pearly-white rows of teeth are, indeed, revealed, but, however beautiful, they're saw-edged and sharp, the canines like Turkish daggers. Its hands – the forepaws – and feet are large; in fact, considering the size of the body, rather like a lynx's paws. And, while its fur coat has from time to time looked tangled, its head is not crowned with dangling hair. It has a huge black brush, just as if the hair-stylist who created Tina Turner's image had a salon in the forest.

I leaf through more of *Pessi and Illusia*. The animals and the plants chat away like anything, and then a cutesy little girl appears, whose eyes are big and blue and amazingly bright and who has white curly hair like a cloudlet on a sunny day. A fairy.

The troll and the fairy introduce themselves to each other: they are Pessi and Illusia – not difficult to work out, considering the title of the book. One is a pessimist, and the other lives in the land of illusion – clever old Kokko! And because both their names are diminutives, because of their small size, Illusia establishes that they're fated to be companions in destiny . . .

I shut the book. Thoughts go whizzing through my head.

So what does the troll mean for me?

A protégé, somewhat like a pigeon with a broken wing? Or an exotic pet? Or maybe a stranger on a short visit, rather oddly behaved but altogether captivating, who'll be leaving one day when the time's right?

Or what?

I ask myself and give no reply.

I reach out and grasp the next book.

A.W. Chalmers, *The Hidden Trails of Mankind*, 1985

For the most part, the ancestors of man may well have adapted flexibly without the constant need for major mutations; but more drastic environmental changes called for more pronounced mutations. Since the close of the Miocene period there have been two such major evolutionary leaps.

The first occurred when Australopithecus experienced a restructuring of the pelvis and the foot, which allowed a brachiating forest ape to become a more-or-less upright walker. This four-limbed 'southern ape' thus became two-legged, with hands free for manipulation, as did, convergently, Felipithecus, the so-called 'cat-ape'. Both Australopithecus and Felipithecus probably carried loads. Upright walking and the development of the deltoid muscle would allow the bearing of weights, such as tools, food and children, from one place to another.

Approximately four million years later the second important hominid mutation occurred. This was the rapid expansion of the brain, leading to the emergence of Cro-Magnon Man, classified as the species *Homo sapiens*, the species we ourselves belong to.

Angel

It stands in a museum display-cabinet on the ground floor of the library, looking like a streamlined thundercloud. Its coat has lost much of its shiny black during the years spent in the glass case. To suggest the beast's environment, it's been surrounded by a miscellany of foliage, lichen and musty-looking plastic stones. The taxidermist has stuffed it in a slightly crouching position, and the long and supple fingers on the forelimbs stretch towards the glass, so that as you approach the cabinet you're startled and take an instinctive step backwards. Its muzzle is creased into a sneer, and the strikingly large teeth are dark yellow – perhaps because of long conservation. I observe that the taxidermist was incorrectly informed about trolls' eyes. To catch the fury and danger of the animal it has been given brown glass-button eyes, which give it a sad, lost look. These might be suitable for a bear, say, but are totally unlike the troll's actual eyes, which are large, fiery slant eyes with irises that are vertical stripes. I press my hands and nose and lips to the glass. It mists over by my mouth as I whisper, 'Help me.'

A.W. Chalmers, *The Hidden Trails of Mankind*, 1985

At the close of the Miocene period salt began to be concentrated in salt basins, and there was a global decrease in oceanic salinity. In consequence, the Antarctic seas began to ice over, doubling the size of the ice cap and lowering sea levels worldwide. The trees began to diminish in size and the African rain forest shrank in extent, leaving only smaller areas where the arboreal apes are still to be found. The eastern side of the continent became a savannah of grass country, though dotted with woodland. This savannah experienced alternating wet and dry seasons, times of abundance and times of dearth, seasons of flood and seasons of cracked mud. The upright two-limb carriage of the hominid Australopithecus allowed its adaptation to this new environment. No longer confined to trees, the hominid was no longer dependent on them.

A similar convergent-evolutionary adaptation occurred in another mammal, the 'cat-ape' Felipithecus, bred in the South-East Asian jungle. The broad shoulders, long arms and partly prehensile toes of both Australopithecus and Felipithecus suggest that both animals still resorted on occasion, perhaps for refuge, to trees. But with the declining availability of trees Felipithecus had to adapt to a new and variable terrain. In search of food, it sought a new home in the East Asian plains and finally the Siberian forests.

Palomita

The stairwell's a big, listening ear, with the bell echoing ring-ring-ring, fainter and fainter, until it disappears. I'm at Mikael's door, but Mikael's not at home. I've checked the time: it's the same as when I last met him, but anyway he's not here. I couldn't check through the peep-hole in the door to see if he was coming, as I'd had to clean the flat and do a lot of washing, and the noise of the washing-machine drowns the footsteps from the stairwell.

But now there's a sound below, and I turn, and my heart starts racing – and I can't tell if it's fear or a vain hope. That friendly fast-talking woman who lives opposite us is coming up the stairs, though she doesn't live on this floor. I could easily fit into one of her trouser-legs. Pentti got her to open the door of our flat one day when he'd lost his jacket with the keys in the pocket. She always wears the same trouser-suit with thick checks sewn on, and she has large dangling earrings. She asks me what I want Mikael for, smiling with her head on one side as if she really wanted to be friendly, while her question sounds rather cross.

Mikael's been around to our flat and put a brand-new, expensive Spanish-language colour magazine through the letterbox. It was a good thing Pentti wasn't at home when he brought it. Mikael had stuck a little card on the cover with a paper clip, saying 'Thanks for the help' in English and some rather funny-looking Spanish, and he'd signed it Mikael. Mikael, not Miguel. Mikael obviously thought I knew Spanish well, though I can't read more than a few words. Very few Filipinos still speak Spanish. Actually, I can't read very much English either. But the magazine pictures are beautiful and glossy.

I don't, of course, tell her all this but point to the catfood tin and the door. It won't fit through the letterbox; it's too fat. I've wrapped a piece of paper around it, fastened with a rubber band. It says, 'For your cat. Thanks for the magazine, Palomita.' The woman bows low like a checked mountain. She speaks a very slow Finnish, carefully twisting her mouth on each word. I realize she's saying I must come again some other time, or would I like her to deliver the package instead. She holds out her hand, with its tight rings. I shake my head. I don't want to give the tin away. Getting the money together has taken me a long time. I've hidden the magazine in the clothes basket. Pentti never touches the clothes basket.

The woman goes, winking sympathetically. I hurry into the flat. I'll have to hide the catfood tin as well, until another time.

Angel

I don't know what I expected to find in the library. A beautiful shiny-backed reference book, perhaps, called *The Domestic Feeding of Wild Beasts*? And all I'd have to do would be look down the index alphabetically: ape, bear, lynx, pine marten – ah, there it is – troll. And then off to the market hall to do the shopping.

I go back to the library's computer to see if I've missed anything. One reference is curious – to the Children's Music Department? I sigh and tap in for more precise information. And there it is, the silly song, and the words.

As soon as I see the piece the music begins to pound in my head. I know it off by heart, like every other Finn, even though I've never actually *listened* to it. Not until now, when I let the corny tune and words grind around my head as if it were a jukebox.

> Would you keep a bandersnatch
> if only you could catch it?
> Put it in a basket
> and dare to fetch it home?

My heart's pounding away to the beat of the ghastly diddy-dah refrain, when the piece hops cheerfully on to this:

> But where's the mum who'll let you take
> a troll back home to sleep?
> Might as well ask Mum to keep
> a sewer rat or a snake.

> Dah dah diddy dah, diddy diddy day.

The music in my head suddenly switches off. I realize I've been thinking a sewer rat or a snake, a sewer rat or a snake . . . And those words, pointing to something well known, about two things that belong together, and in a certain way . . . provide the solution.

Selma Lagerlöf, 'The Changeling', from *Trolls and Humans*, 1915

'I've no idea what kind of food to give a changeling,' she told her husband. 'It won't eat anything I put in front of it.'

'Well, that's no surprise, is it?' he said. 'Haven't you heard? Trolls don't eat anything but frogs and mice.'

'But surely you're not going to ask me to go fishing in the pond for frogs?'

'Of course not. Best let it die of hunger.'

Angel

I open the shop door. A tiny bell tinkles. The door closes.

I greet the shopkeeper. I point one out. The shopkeeper asks me questions I don't hear properly. I shake my head. It doesn't matter, it's all the same. His eyebrows go up. It doesn't matter?

He gathers up a pile of supplementary products – I'll need this, all the same, I'll need that, and this. My denials are in vain. I pick up the box and push a note into his hand, get my change and a receipt.

The little bell tinkles.

C.B. Gaunitz and Bo Rosen,
The Animal Book: 'Vertebrates', 1962

Animals that prey on one another have to be able to bite and use their claws. They also have to be swift, cunning and extremely patient.

The fox is known to be a crafty hunter, the wolf a persevering pursuer – it may follow its prey for miles on end. The lynx lurks in ambush with unbelievable persistence, the troll moves more quietly than a shadow, and the otter is a swift and skilful swimmer.

The more exclusively an animal feeds on meat the sharper its front molars are and the more persevering it is by nature. The weasel is amusingly inquisitive, but at the same time so indomitable it will attack a much larger animal than itself, and it does not fear man if its nest is disturbed.

The badger and the bob-tailed bear are choosy: they will settle only for the choicest delicacies of the flora and fauna. Like true gourmets they particularly relish strong-flavoured food, even rotting meat. Also, the furtive troll can occasionally be sidetracked by a carcass, but in general it is more selective about its food.

Angel

I open the box and let the guinea-pig out on to the floor.

I shut my eyes because I can't believe I'm really doing this. The guinea-pig is soft and smooth-haired and warm; its pink nose trembles and its whiskers quiver. It's white with brown patches. In fact it's quite horribly cute.

Cute enough to eat.

Martes

The telephone rings a fair few times before Mikael replies. When he does finally pick up the receiver, he's out of breath, gulping and coughing.

'Been throwing up?' I ask teasingly.

'Who's that?' His voice is agitated.

'Martti.'

'Martes.' He breathes the name. He didn't believe I'd ever phone. He doesn't thank me for the last time we met, and he doesn't apologize for his behaviour. A good sign; he doesn't want to remember all that. I've been racking my brains to think of someone else I could call about this but couldn't come up with anyone.

I hate needing anyone.

Above all, I hate needing a person I wasn't expecting ever to speak to again. Actually, though, the fact that he needs me too, that what I have to say matters to him, eases the awful dread that he might take my call the wrong way. Instinctively I distance myself, draw the bait further off.

'You in a hurry? You sound it. I can ring later.'

'No, no. I've nothing special on. Let rip.'

I can hear background noises, sudden odd rustlings and snappings, randomly rhythmical.

'Could be I've got a project for you. How're you fixed for work?'

There's a loud scraping, as if someone's dragging a metal fork over the floor or the bathroom tiles. A thump. Another thump.

'Couple of small jobs this week, then more space in my diary. Okay?'

Two lightning scraping noises.

'You're free at the beginning of next week?'

'First thing Monday morning, if you like. So what time –?'

A scraping, a thump, a shrill squeak, and Mikael breaks off, drawing in a quick startled breath.

'What on earth's going *on* there?'

Mikael breathes deeply twice. 'I'm, ah, watching . . . this video . . . kind of experimental effort. Rather lurid effects right now.'

'Oh? What genre?'

'Well, let's say . . . horror.'

Angel

When I get back home with a fresh pile of books, euphoric about my coming meeting with Martes – now so soon, so soon – the first thing that happens is that I step on a troll turd. Let anyone dare to moan to me about miserable homecomings – the kids have been making sticky toffee in the kitchen and not cleaned up, their husband's flat on the sofa, pissed out of his mind – well, none of them has to step on trollshit in their own hallway. Naturally, the shit's been neatly pushed under the doormat so my weight squashes it out on to both the underside and the parquet.

Just for a change, the troll's not lying on the bed but on the floor, idly giving the odd shake to the rubber mouse I've bought it – of which there's precious little left, just a greyish torso. It's in languid mood, with lack-lustre eyes, though presumably no longer hungry. Of course I know it's a passive creature in the daytime, but it rarely moves now, even at night.

Did you have to give it solid food? a mean little voice in my head asks when I grab a dustpan and some kitchen towels, trying not to breathe through my nose as I scrape the shit into the rubbish. I try not to look at it, for I know what it's made of. I don't want to see any little bones or brown-white tufts of hair.

Back in the living-room my voice is genuinely angry: 'Who's been doing a poo on the floor?'

The troll glances at me and unconcernedly turns its head away. The toy mouse interests it much more. I've bought some cat litter and put it in a box in a corner of the bathroom, but the troll doesn't show any interest. Peeing it does, for some reason, on the bathroom floor, perhaps because it did it there in the first place and has somehow marked it out territorially – and anyway the puddles are easy to swill into the drain in the floor. But with this demonshit dilemma I'm truly stuck.

'What are we going to do with you, Pessi?' I sigh, and several seconds go by before I realize I've given him a name.

'A Tale of a Bear and a Troll', Inari-Lapp folklore, collected and published by A.V. Koskimies and T. Itkonen, *Proceedings of the Finno-Ugrian Society, XI,* 1917

Walking in the forest one day, a troll came across a bear, who was digging a winter den for himself. The troll asked the bear, 'What are you doing?' The bear said, 'Escaping from man.' The troll replied, 'I don't expect to find any man I need be afraid of.' The bear said, 'You have to fear man because he has weapons. Take a walk down the main road and you'll find a man to fear.' The troll set off walking down the road. He met a young boy. He asked him, 'Are you a man?' The boy replied, 'I'm not a man, just the start of one.' The troll passed the boy by and continued down the road. Now an old man came along and the troll asked him, 'So you're a man, aren't you?' The old man replied, 'I'm not a man. I've been a man, but I'm not one any more.' The troll passed him by, too, set off down the road again, walked and walked, until he met a soldier, riding on a horse. The troll asked him, 'So you *are* a man, aren't you?' The soldier replied, 'A man you called me, and a man I am.' Then the troll curled his claws and started to go for him. The soldier grabbed his gun and shot the troll's tail, blowing the hairs off, leaving a mere tuft at the end. The troll swung his head around, intending to bite the soldier, but the soldier pulled out his sword and scratched an upright scratch on each of the troll's eyes. The troll had to take to his heels, and he went back the way he came until he met the bear again. The bear said, '*Now* do you believe that men are to be feared?' The troll did believe, and he built himself a winter den, too, as he's done every winter ever since.

Angel

This biologist I'm consulting over the phone has swallowed my story, that I'm a journalist working on a story about trained animals. He supposes my topic touches on circus ethics – a brilliant cover I'd never have hit on myself – and he's already been through elephants, bears and sea-lions.

'You often see trained lions and tigers,' I say, leading him on. 'What about the indigenous animals of Finland? Do you consider one could systematically train a bear, for instance, or even . . . a troll?' I ask lightly, in passing.

The Prof delivers a long lecture, from which I gather chiefly that wolves, for instance, are extremely trainable, because they're pack animals, a subject on which the cursed Grzimek, whose name the old fart spells out for me with excruciating care, letter by letter, has carried out proper research. And they obey the individual who has authority, even if it's a man. The relation to feline animals, such as lions and tigers, is different: cats are usually extremely independent and won't do anything without immediate reward. The bottom line is that everything depends on the animals' social norms.

'Social norms?' My tone of voice is emphatically enquiring, like a second-rate actor's.

'Well, we do have very little information on the subject of trolls. One theory suggests that they possibly live in a sort of micro-troop, like a pride of lions, and in such troops a certain hierarchical behaviour-pattern operates. On the other hand, the tiger, for example, is a territorial animal: it hunts alone and is intolerant of other individuals in its own territory. There remains, of course, a possibility, too, that trolls maintain an alpha-male order, like that of chimpanzees, making for a comparatively disorganized-seeming troop dominated by a large male. This means the alpha has primary sexual rights over the troop's females, and so on. At present, the entire basis for this hypothesis rests on the speculation that the convergence of the trolls' evolution with that of the primates may have operated on other dimensions besides outward appearance . . .'

I'm not much the wiser, but then the old boy's voice seems to perk up.

'But the best results are always achieved when the animal's trained at the cub stage. Rewards and punishments in suitable proportions . . . I remember talk of a trained troll that was sometimes seen in the market, a little before the war, obviously the same one that's now stuffed in the Tampere Biological Museum . . .'

I shiver as I remember the faded animal in the glass display-cabinet and its total degradation. A trained troll.

'Large predators are currently an unusually popular subject, in the wake of the happenings in Joensuu and Kuopio . . .'

Joensuu and Kuopio? I ask myself, without knowing what he's talking about.

'Which journal are you writing for?' he asks, but I'm already putting the phone down.

'Wild Beasts Haunt Our Cities', *Finnish Evening News* (30 November 1999)

The people of Kuopio and Joensuu have become anxious about large predators being seen near the towns, and they are not alone. In recent weeks there have even been sightings outside certain central and southern Finnish towns. After the many previous sightings of bears and wolves, urban areas are now being approached by trolls.

Trolls are rarely sighted in Finland, but recently, over a short period, half-a-dozen very reliable sightings have occurred near the eastern frontier, some very close to housing.

The troll, usually an extremely shy animal, has been extending its habitat from the uninhabited forests and fields and moving closer to towns. Some attribute this to food shortages. People living near large forests have been advised to keep their dustbins tightly closed and their small pets locked in. Trolls rarely attack human beings, so there is no cause for alarm; and, being night creatures, they are likely to be encountered only very late or in the early hours.

Pets are disturbed

'My Alsatian started a terrible howling,' says Risto Huttula of Kuopio. 'I've never heard it howl before. I went out into the yard and tried to calm the dog down, but it wouldn't be calmed.' Then Huttula noticed two coal-black, two-legged creatures running along the edge of a field. Obviously the dog had caught the scent on the wind before the creatures were visible. Foresters went to investigate the traces, but on the almost snowless ground they found no hard evidence. Were the figures trolls that had postponed their hibernation or clandestine intruders in the forest?

The neighbour's Bernese mountain dog had whined and padded restlessly back and forth throughout the previous night. In the morning the dog refused to follow the tracks, rejecting all incentives.

Pulliainen's yes to 'urban animals'

Biologist Professor Erkki Pulliainen considers the situation transitory and no cause for alarm.

'The situation does occur sporadically with the first snows and the onset of the hibernation season for bears and trolls. The only disturbances for city-dwellers at such times', Pulliainen emphasizes, 'are likely to be from wolves, wolverines and lynxes, and these haunt the neighbouring terrain only in search of food, with no intention of deliberately intruding on people.' The food-shortage theory is not accepted by Pulliainen personally.

'On the contrary, the reason for the animals' resort to city outskirts is clearly that certain small parasitical animals are likely to be plentiful in precisely these areas. And the lynx, for example, has shown itself over the course of time to be, as a species, highly culturally adaptable.' Lynxes have long been present on the outskirts of Helsinki, Turku and Tampere, Pulliainen reports, where plentiful food is available, such as hares and white-tailed reindeer, and the terrain is suitable: marshland coppices, dense mixed woodland and coniferous forest.

The locals are in fear

Riikka Vesaisto, a Joensuu farmer's wife, totally disagrees with Professor Pulliainen. In her view, large wild beasts are a concrete threat, not only to her sheep but to her family.

'Two weeks ago my son was off to school – he's in the first form – and he said he'd seen an "old black man" staring at him from behind a fir tree. The lad ran for it and managed to get to the school playground without being hurt. Together we checked an animal book and found out what he'd seen: it was a troll. How long will it have to be before we wake up and realize a full-grown troll is a wild beast two metres tall and that a little child's just a snack for it?'

Riikka Vesaisto's husband Antti shares her view.

'They ought to bring bounty money back. Of course they're all going on about nature preservation now, but I'd like to see that greengage's face if some wolf or bugaboo snapped up his own brat on the way to school.'

Angel

Monday. Tomorrow's Monday.

He could have been ringing others. I've no idea how much I can hope for any more. Myself, I daren't make a move; but ring he bloody well did.

Pessi's learned to be wary of newspapers. I've never actually hit him, only slapped at him symbolically, but he clearly knows that a rolled-up newspaper symbolizes the authority of the alpha. Now that he's quietly begun to grasp that I don't like trollshit under the doormat, he's been resorting in need to the box in the corner of the bathroom, where I've been putting cut-up advertising sheets and other junk paper. I've got to change the contents every day, otherwise he won't use it again. I tried scented cat litter, but that, for some reason, he absolutely detests.

As sweeteners to the rolled-up newspaper I've been manipulating Pessi with gerbils and white mice. I've been giving him titbits like these when he's been a well-behaved little trollboy – and gerbils are not nearly as expensive or poo-generating as guinea-pigs or hamsters.

Though he eats now and then, and can even be bothered to play at hunting the animals, he's not in good condition. I've wondered whether those budding juvenile offenders hurt him in some way. Has he got fractures somewhere or even internal bleeding? But I'd have noticed something in the way he moves if he had muscle or leg pains. Yet he's languid and subdued most of the time, like a fluttering candle flame.

When he does make one of his rare moves, he's supple, like quick-silver. He seems to be reversing gravity. His total muscular capacity is enormous, considering his size. He moves about like oil, as if made of silk.

His eyes are full of nocturnal wildfire.

Part 2

There Flared a Wondrous Glow of Light

Martes

'Calvin Klein?' I ask and lean towards Mikael, my nose almost touching his hair. His pale cheeks flush. He's not been sleeping.

'What?'

'Aftershave. You've changed your brand.'

Mikael smells a little of Klein One – spruce, lemon, spices – and something inside me stirs. But when he gives me that puppy-dog look, searching my eyes for something that's not there, he gets on my nerves. I thought I'd made it clear after those two pub sessions that he was barking up the wrong tree. But now I need Mikael, and so I bend towards him and sniff as softly as a horse sensing a shy filly. He's got to remember how much he wants to please me.

'Yes, it's a brand new thing – they were handing out samples at Stockmann's. Whatever. Experimental so far, I believe – not sure whether it'll ever come on to the market properly . . .'

He's so on edge it makes me sick.

'Hey, I've not asked you here to find out what aftershave you're using. I've got a job for you.'

I make it short. It's a denim firm. They're putting us and three other advertising agencies into competition for a new campaign. The name of their jeans series is Stalker, and they of course want to be an instant fashion icon. It's got to brand itself into the consciousness of the fashion police in one single lightning flash. The firm's looking for something about as original and urgent as Diesel and yet socking the unconscious as subliminally as the old MicMac campaigns. But dead new. Of course.

'You've always been one of our best photographers. And recently you've shown what you can do with computerized graphics. Find us an idea.'

'Idea?'

'Naturally I and a couple of other ADs and copy-writers are putting our noses to the grindstone, and smoke's rising from our cerebral lobes. But right now we need every single right and left hemisphere going. Okay, among other things, "Stalker" is about stalking celebrities, but we're not after any stupid Madonna image; we want a brand-new perspective. We want you to come up with some image, something fucking lurid. Along the lines of pouring petrol over the Stalkers in the Jan Palach square in Prague, setting light to them and making the smoke form a slogan like "C'mon, baby, light my fire" – you know the sort of thing. No limit.'

Angel

'I want something strong,' Martes says, and I can't take my eyes off his hands: they're clenching sexily, as if grasping two iron bars. 'Something never seen before and violent.'

When I look up he's noticed I've been staring at his hands, and his eyes narrow as he smiles.

'You've got the sickest imagination I've ever come across. Let loose. Free your mind and send it flying.'

Martes

Mikael nods slowly, and I grab a large heavy sports bag out of the corner.

'Eight pairs of Stalkers here for you, all possible sizes, and you can have more if you need them. There's bags of time. A couple of months. The deadline's the end of March. And if the idea sees the light of day, it'll mean loads of dosh for you. We're talking thousands.'

And if the idea sees the light of day, and if we get the commission, it'll mean at least a quarter of a million euros for us. But that I don't say. I chuck the bag into Mikael's arms, he almost flops down under the weight of it, but with a couple of steps backwards he remains on his feet. 'Our rock and standby. Suppose you know your nickname here?'

Mikael's hanging on to the bag with both hands. He looks up enquiringly.

I lower my voice almost to a whisper: 'Michelangelo.'

Angel

Michelangelo.

I wasn't Michelangelo when we first met, I was Studio Hartikainen.

And I still am Studio Hartikainen, the advertising photographer, graphic designer and computer artist. And he's Martti, Martes, the hardest AD in the city's toughest advertising office.

I remember.

I come into the office and introduce myself. I show my portfolio and worm my way into the talk about diffusers and image data banks. Immediately an easy, streamlined trust springs up between Martes and me.

Trust, yes, and of course mutual admiration: the way a competent professional can admire another whose field is close enough for him to have the requisite understanding for admiration but distant enough to eliminate competition for the same clients.

I remember, Martes.

I remember how, during the consultation, you gave me eye contact behind our shared customer's back and pulled a face in just the way we both understand, and I nearly burst out laughing.

I remember that once, planning a visualization together, it was breathtaking how we saw totally eye to eye, how one of us had only to say half a word and the other's face lit up, and he said, 'Yes! – I was just about to say that myself!' And we hit high five, and I remember your face and your look and your denim shirt's top button unfastened.

I remember how, when we were alone together, I sometimes noticed you looking at me closely, so closely I began to get breathless, and our glances lingered a little too long, making my voice go husky as I explained something. And I read your eyes, Martes, there was no lie in them. There was no pretence in them.

I remember you inviting me to consultations, though things could have been fixed over the phone. I remember your asking me now and then to have a pint with you after work. We spoke about everything under the sun, and we respected each other and admired each other and liked each other and laughed at the same things, and – oh, we were on the same wavelength, to the millihertz! And maybe we drank a glass or two more than we should.

I remember feeling your chest in my arms, feeling your erection through your trousers as we leaned against the Tammerkoski River railings that dark night. I can still feel your mouth on mine, Martes, tasting of cigarettes and Guinness, your moustache roughing my upper lip, and it makes me feel faint.

Martes, I remember, and I know still that it wasn't my imagination.

Palomita

In the little well there's a reward.

First I hear footsteps, and I hope and hope and hope until the sides of my neck hurt. He's climbing the steps in the peephole. He's a little doll walking across the surface of my eye. He has a big shopping bag on his shoulder. I slither off like a lizard into the bathroom. There's a tin of catfood in the washing basket. Pentti's snores come through the bedroom wall, as if someone were scratching a sack with their broken nails. I've unplugged the telephone and put the mobile under a pile of pillows on the sofa so he won't wake. The third time it was difficult for him to get a hard-on, and I was afraid he'd notice I was purposely trying to tire him out. Sometimes he's given me a beating, because it's obviously my fault if he can't get a hard-on, but this time fortunately he just growled and told me to suck him off, and I got him so pumped out I knew he'd sleep like the dead for the next two hours.

My hands have to be feathers so the door won't click when I shut it. I fly up the stairs without a sound. His door's just about to swallow him up when I whisper his name.

Angel

'Mikael.'

I hear someone breathing my name on the stairs behind, and I turn in surprise. It's the postal-purchase bride from downstairs. She's waving something cylindrical, and she's in the doorway before I can react properly. My mind races for a moment but then calms down. It's daytime, Pessi's sleeping, and besides he's becoming so feeble it makes me weep. Some days he'll only lap up a little water, even if I've bought him a gerbil or hamster, and the sparkle has gone out of his eyes. The living-room door's closed, so I let the woman into the hall, because clearly she doesn't want to stand on the stairway: she almost pushes in past me.

The woman – Palomita, she says – explains something in poor English. It takes a moment before I can make any sense of it. She wants to thank me for the magazine I gave her, and this is a gift in return, something for my cat.

For my cat? Quite.

I thank her, smiling more from a wretched sense of the ridiculous than pleasure in the gift, and she stares movingly up at me with her big brown roe-deer's eyes. Then she suddenly gives a start, and her eyes widen.

There are footsteps on the stairway.

They're obviously coming up. My flat's the only one on the top floor. The original two-room flat next door is now my studio, so that someone, whoever it may be, is on their way here – nowhere else.

Palomita

The footsteps come up the stairs like blows. They strike through the door into my ears and face. The worst moment is when they reach Mikael's door. The pain when it actually hits you isn't nearly so bad as dreading it coming.

I'm a lizard seeking a hole behind Mikael and then behind a coat. The footsteps stop, and the no-sound now is a lot more frightening than the sound was.

I don't want to breathe. Soon there'll be the buzz of the doorbell. Soon Pentti will be hammering on the door with his fists. He'll shout and swear – words with sharp corners – and his face'll go from red to blue. My legs throw me out of the coat – somewhere else, to a door, I'm hanging on its handle, I'm deep in another room that's flooded in light.

Angel

There's a cough and an almost inaudible bump of a plastic bucket, showing that it's the old woman from the ground floor, cleaning the stairs. But the sound of her steps has turned Palomita into a hyperactive whirlwind. First she jumps behind me to hide, then she conceals herself among the coats hanging in the hall, and then she takes a hopeless dive towards the sitting-room door, and 'Hey, don't go in there' is the only thing I can get out, before she's opened the door and come to a stop on the threshold, her mouth open.

Palomita

It's very quiet. My own breathing's like a breeze going through my head. Then I hear footsteps starting again and fading away. It can't have been Pentti. Pentti would have come right in through Mikael's door.

Mikael's standing in his hall, holding the catfood tin. His face seems to be saying I've done something that's not right. Or he has. Now that I know the steps can't have been Pentti's I can take in what I saw before. I go closer to the white leather sofa, which is like a pale smooth-skinned mushroom that has bulged up out of the floor. The cat's really big and pitch-black all over. It's bigger than most dogs. It's not asleep, its eyes are open and its ears are moving, but it doesn't even raise its head.

I go closer still.

'It's sick, real sick,' I say.

At home in Malayali there were a lot of dogs and cats and other animals wandering around our house. When an animal looks like that it'll die soon.

I touch it. It feels bony and hot and its fur is full of little tangles and knots. Its nostrils spread and tremble, my smell's new to it. Its face isn't catlike, more like an ape's. Or a person's.

Mikael asks me, in a tense whisper, to be careful.

'It's not a cat; it's a troll,' he says. I don't know the word troll, but I realize he's telling me it's actually a wild animal, a cub he's found.

'And he hasn't eaten anything for two days.' Mikael's voice can hardly be heard.

'He's really sick,' I say again.

I remember what I did when I found the dog's den under the house. I don't know how it finally turned out with the puppies, as the letter from Manila had come already, and my father and brother were taking me the next morning to Zamboanga and putting me on the ship from Cotabato. They told me I was going to be a nurse. I was delighted, because I thought I'd do well as that. After all, I'd just been caring for small still-blind puppies whose mother had been run over by a jeep.

I take hold of the catfood tin and gesture with it, until Mikael goes into the kitchen, and I hear the sound of the tin-opener. He comes back with it open. I push my finger in and curl it. The catfood's like thick coarse mud. I hold my finger out carefully in front of the troll's mouth, and he pulls his head weakly back, frightened, his round head trembling like a cat's. I breathe on my finger, warming the food and putting my own smell on it. I hold my finger out again, and now the troll sniffs it, suspiciously. But then a small pink tongue comes out of its lips, and he gives a lick. Once. Twice.

I burst out laughing with triumph, and because the tongue's tickling my finger. I meet Mikael's astonished look.

'He's never eaten catfood before.'

'Perhaps we must give it like this. He thinks I'm his *mamà*.'

I don't know if Mikael understands, but his eyes are unbelieving, delighted, covering the wild distress beneath.

Michael watches while the troll eats a few pats of the brown paste. Then the troll shuts his eyes, leaving just a shining line between the lids. He hasn't felt well enough to clean his eyes; there are little yellow specks in the corners. I get up, hand the tin to Mikael and go off to wash my hand in the kitchen sink. Mikael follows me.

'Thanks a million,' he says. I shrug and raise my eyebrows: no big deal. But I'm prouder and happier than ever before in this country.

Mikael puts the tin on the washstand and, to my surprise, takes my hands in his, squeezing them and raising them to his chest. 'Thank you,' he says again. And, scared, I swing around, resisting, and disappear into the hall, quick as a shadow. But before I can squeeze the door sound-lessly shut behind me, I can't help glancing back at the kitchen door: Mikael's standing there with a look I can't understand on his face, and my heart thumps, thumps, faster than it has for a long, long time.

Angel

No, Pessi's not well. He eats and drinks and empties his bowels, but he's not well. His coat doesn't shine, there's no fire in his eyes, he plays without enthusiasm. He sleeps day and night – as if in a fever.

I myself hardly eat or sleep, my hold on work's gone. Routine stuff goes forward but nothing particularly creative. The Stalkers Martes gave me lie about in a corner. That damned jeans deadline seems far off, but in practice it's only a few weeks away.

Palomita realized as soon as she saw Pessi.

Something has to be done. Soon.

Ecke

I've got a box seat; the only thing that's missing is a pair of opera glasses, and the drama's first-class home-TV soap. Angel and Dr Spiderman are sitting in the Café Bongo's back room. Together. I'm not the only one following the action. It's the most interesting thing that's happened in this mangy dump for a long time.

Angel's eagerly telling the tale to Spiderman, gesticulating, going on about something of the utmost importance and occasionally letting his hand rest casually on Spider's arm. Spider's narrow hound-dog face is wearing a disbelieving expression that continually veers towards the euphoric. He's been thinking that this Angel was as far out of his reach as one dancing on a pinhead.

In the days when Angel dumped Spider, someone saw Angel in some pub or other with a peculiar bearded weirdo, goggled and hairy, not one of us. A nasty rumour had it that Angel was making an all-out pass at a hetero. But here he is, rubbing up the Doctor as if nothing has happened.

Angel Hartikainen. His real first name I'm sure I've never even heard. A man of thirty, he still has a seventeen-year-old cherub's face, crowned with a golden cloud of curls, and not a tiny hint of receding temples.

It's a knife-thrust in my belly. Ever since I first saw Angel I've known I want him.

Dr Spiderman

His golden head bends closer to me, so I catch the scent of his aftershave. It's a new one on me, woodlandish and metallic, strangely arousing.

Angel's telling a long, meandering tale, the purpose of which is beyond me. He seasons his story with lively details and finally arrives, with conspicuous casualness, at the main point: that his uncle has somewhere found a wolverine's cub – or was it a lynx's kitten? – and brought it home and fed it, and it's pissed in a corner, ha ha, and then they've got it to eat something, but it's nevertheless rather listless, apathetic, weary, dull-coated. For ages apparently they've been wondering what on earth's bothering the creature. And Angel's leaning his head my way as if expecting me to join in on the idiotic affair.

'My Angel, since when have you supposed that a veterinary surgeon's idea of fun and relaxation consists in listening to guff about some sick specimen of nature?' I ask. Angel doesn't relent.

'Well, he can't contact the zoo. He mightn't be given permission to keep a wild animal, so . . . They're just . . . thinking . . . about . . . what might be up with it.'

'No wonder they haven't sorted that out, since they haven't even found out whether it's a wolverine or a lynx.'

'Well, that's me – not remembering! It's some predatory animal, a large one – what sorts are there? Or does that make a big difference in deciding what's up with it?'

I bang my beermug on the table. Clearly Angel's determined to go on about his uncle's wolverine the whole evening, unless I produce an opinion.

'Not necessarily. Generally speaking, every single wild animal is carrying some sort of internal parasite. A full-grown animal hardly notices it, but it may well weaken a cub.'

Angel's eyes light up. He pulls his chair still closer to me, as if I'd begun talking about some exotic and slightly perverse sexual technique. The fellow gets a real kick out of internal parasites, I reflect, taken aback.

'In all probability it's roundworm,' I go on, and Angel drinks in every word from my lips. And in the midst of my astonishment I begin to be very amused. 'The whipworm and hookworm are possible but rare. It could be a beef tapeworm, but the roundworm is the most common. It's found regularly in all the large predators.'

'So where would it have picked it up?'

'From its mother. A parasite in an inactive state passes into the young through the blood circulation in the placenta, and hormonal activity then wakes it up, as it were. In other words, the disease is unpreventable in advance. A cub in poor condition can grow tired and be in poor shape, even die.'

'I suppose it can be treated?'

'I'd think your uncle is a bit late with his animal: it's either got better by itself by now, or otherwise your uncle may have got some new but not particularly fine-quality wolverine mittens.'

Angel closes his eyes slowly, as if he were trying with all his might to control himself.

'If you were treating roundworm, what would you do?'

'I'd administer an anthelmintic.'

Angel's lips move. He shapes the word silently: an . . . thel . . . MIN . . . tic . . . an . . . thel . . . MIN . . . tic. Memorizing it. I've no idea what he's going to do with the knowledge. Is he going to rush off and save his uncle's illegal wolverine? But anyway I add fuel to the fire.

'Mebendazole is the commercial form. It's a wonderful medicament. In practice it works on all animals. You can employ it just as well with reindeer and cattle as with the large predators.'

Angel's eyes blaze up with interest. I smile.

'Unfortunately, you can't get it from the chemist.'

He swallows the bait and takes the hook, which will give me two different catches. And of those two, satisfaction of curiosity is almost as pleasurable as satisfied lust.

Angel

Another thing I've managed to extract from Spider is that this anthelmintic takes two or three weeks to have effect and that the extermination of the parasite's no big deal: the animal doesn't, thank God, throw up or excrete strings of worms wriggling in a pool of bile but little by little gets better. He also drops the hint in passing that it's a common type of medicine he himself always keeps in his store.

Lightly brushing Dr Spiderman's thighs with my fingertips, I breathe inviting little sighs towards him and let my eyes dissolve in his. I say that I've been longing for him.

And, feverishly, I'm thinking how I can get him to make love at the practice and not at his home? It's not beyond possibility: we've done it before, on the gaudy sofa in his waiting-room. Remembering that helps – and instantly it tells me which string to pull.

'Do you still remember our first time?'

Spiderman nods, with a strange look in his eyes.

'That creaky waiting-room sofa, with dog hairs everywhere. You said the cleaner wouldn't be there till Sunday . . . And then you brought out that bizarre collar! A restraining collar!'

I laugh boisterously, far more than the unforgettably daft event deserves.

'I was still picking those dog hairs off my underpants all the next week. And the memory's stayed with me.'

Spider gives a brief dry smile, but I can see he remembers, too, and well.

'I'd give almost anything for that same feeling again. Just that very feeling,' I say and lick my lips lightly and then sink my eyes bashfully in my beermug.

Dr Spiderman

Angel has forced me with a little affectionate flirting to show him my reception-room, as if it were something he'd not seen before, something incredible and wonderful. He's sweetly inquisitive and boyish and wants to see everything, wants to know everything, wants me to open all the doors, and bends to kiss me at exactly the moment when I should be locking the drugs-cabinet.

Angel

I feel like Buster Keaton as I sneak through the dark in my boxer shorts. They're the ones I bought in London, literally 'boxers', covered with pictures of those wrinkle-faced, flop-eared, soft-eyed dogs which resemble a certain canine-faced figure currently lying prone in a deep sleep on the shabby sofa. Before I set off for the Café Bongo I remembered they were Spider's favourite underpants – when I first took my jeans off for him at this very spot, they sparked off that nervous strangled but in its own way sexy cackling that is his trademark. I'm cursing that I don't have Pessi's eyes. I can't even find the door from the waiting-room to the reception-room without bumping my toes on the doorsill, making my eyes flash red amoeba-like flecks for a moment. The drugs-cabinet is dimly outlined at the other end of the room, looking like a big white whale stuck on the wall.

I open the door and the hinges creak, making me nearly wet my pants. My heart tries to jump out of my skin. I freeze. I'm an antique statue, so just carry on with your dream, my dear Spider. I know where the anthelmintic is, because, brimming over with breathless enthusiasm, I asked him about everything possible, including whether the medicines were arranged from A to Z or according to their use.

The package is already in my hand when I hear a voice behind me.

'The loo isn't that way.'

If my pulse was fast, it now bursts into a gallop, nearly suffocating me. I try to keep my back to him and stuff the package in my boxers. It mustn't slip down through the legholes, so I'm forced to squeeze the square cardboard box into the fork of my groin, with my balls wedging it in. I turn and try to behave naturally.

'Oh yes, it was that other door.'

'Henrik Tikkanen's writer-friend, Benedict Zilliacus, as I remember, once peed into a blue-painted basketwork chair because he thought it was the sea,' Spider reports from the darkness in his dry voice. He's still on the sofa and won't be able to see any more of me in the darkness than my faintly visible pale-coloured doggie-pants.

I try to walk to the loo without my gait betraying at every step that the excruciatingly sharp corners are poking into the soft flesh of my crotch. I don't know how successful I was, but thank God my denim shirt's over a chair back on the way there, and I snatch it up and take it with me, while trying feebly not to slip into an apelike shuffle. And soon the loo door is shut behind me – and my denim shirt has pockets.

Ecke

Bluesbooze is never a good idea, but anyway the fourth black-dog glass has come to my table, as if by itself, since Angel and Spiderman left. I've given two refusals and turned off one eager raconteur and decided to decamp into the desolation of my own pad – after this fourth drink, of course, just as I did after the second and third – when someone asks if they can sit at my table.

There don't seem to be any empty seats anywhere else, so my companion's clearly forced to sit with me out of sheer necessity, not interest. As it is, that's a pity, for a first glance suggests the guy's agreeable goods: high-calibre brains, tall and broad-shouldered but nevertheless far from being an Atlas-type, with round spectacles, moustache, a full well-tended beard, dark brown slightly curly hair, longish at the neck, and, of course, an earring. Agreeable goods? No, by God. A second and third look, and the guy's *the* catch of the month.

We toss a few ideas around, and then he makes a move that catches me pants down: he asks if I've happened to see Angel. At first I'm completely bemused, as he's using the first name Mikael, but then he uses the more usual Michelangelo, and, God, I come out in goose pimples when he says it. But after describing a few identifying features – fair curly hair, tall, eyes like pieces of sky – I recognize Angel. I let it out that I've seen him but say I don't know him except indirectly. He shot off a while ago, I add. I don't go into more exact detail.

The guy introduces himself. He's Martti something, an advertising man. What he wants Angel for is no big deal – no, naturally not, nor for any of us here. He's been trying to ring him, to check up a bit on how some commission's progressing, but Angel's studio hasn't replied, and the mobile's only on the answerphone. Here he confides his wonder that Mikael doesn't keep his mobile on. A freelance ought to be available twenty-four hours a day. And, with that in mind, he decided to see whether Mikael might perhaps be at his local. The commission's important, really important, otherwise he'd not want to pester Mikael – just wanted to sound out how the project was going.

He's completely overdoing it. He's obviously had several already, and something in this picture stinks anyway. Martti's not one of us, not at first glance, but I've seen these tottering-on-the-brink types before. This has to be the hetero that Angel dumped Spider for.

'So you know – Mikael – well, ' I throw out. I'd almost said 'Angel'.

Martti breaks out again into overdone explanations: as good colleagues in a longish collaboration, which led to a closer acquaintance. I greedily pump him for info. Angel comes from somewhere in northern Ostrobothnia, actually almost in Lapland, moved to Tampere as a little kid, went to school there, then got on to the Lahti photography course, then came back here to work. He's a well-known photographer, much in demand, and nowadays as a virtuoso photo creative, a true magician of the Mac, a Freehand fakir and prophet of Photoshop.

Each word proves that Angel is designed for me, tailored for me, meant for me, and that this guy had better not intervene, no way, and therefore I tell Martti confidentially, and as if by the way, that Angel is keeping company with a veterinarian, has been keeping company with him for a long time, and seriously.

Angel

It's night, and the phone's ringing.

Pessi's so sick he doesn't even really prick up his ears, though the dark-room's filled with the piercing noise that goes right through you. At the sixth ring I pick up the receiver.

'Mikael.'

At the other end there's a moment's silence, and then a voice I know, and it's as if someone had slit my belly open with a single slash and hurled iced water on to my hot intestines. Dr Spiderman.

'I hope it's not a collie.'

I can only stammer. 'What?'

'That damned animal you stole my anthelmintic for. Listen. If it's a collie, the Scottish sheepdog, some bloody relative of Lassie, then it has a known central nervous anomaly. It'll die from the anthelmintic.'

'It's not a collie,' I say, and I could bite my tongue off. There's the tiniest little snort of cold, soft laughter from Dr Spiderman.

'So don't get scared either, then, when our friends the parasites die and briskly secrete toxins.'

'Toxins?'

'The beast'll show symptoms of poisoning, but they'll definitely pass.'

I don't know what to say. The anthelmintic package is a light patch on the corner of the table.

'And then one more thing, my Angel . . .'

My heart thumps limply. A criminal charge?

'You could easily have got a medicine to do the same thing from the chemist. It's called Piperazine.'

Dr Spiderman

Angel's almost sobbing into the phone. The cold and furious fire of vengefulness that's been burning in me begins to die down, turning to grey ash. I'm starting to feel tired and old and stupid. I'm in the same painful, exhausted state as when I was still in my marriage and had gone off the deep end with my slightly under ten-year-old sons – lashing out at them and scolding them for mindless things they'd done. I'm just as exhausted and deflated and agonizingly conscious that nothing I've said has hit home, not even dented the surface. In their eyes, the lashings and scoldings weren't legitimate punishments, educational discipline, but pure demonstrations of my malice – a bigger person's arbitrary use of power and sheer badness – leaving me with nothing but the fear: *can they love me any more after this*?

Why am I ringing in the middle of the night? Why didn't I wait until the next time I saw Angel in the Café Bongo? Then I could have brought the theft of the medicine forward in the most compromising light, making it a merciless counterblow to the pain he's caused, a delicious weapon, an instrument of power.

Because I remember. I'm remembering subliminally a certain other conversation of ours. And now I go cold in real earnest.

'Angel. Listen. If it has . . . if the animal has . . . intestinal parasites, there are bound to be external parasites as well. Fleas or lice, or at least their eggs. Get some Program tablets from the chemist's.'

'Program.'

His voice shows he's mechanically fixing the name in his memory.

'It's easy to use, one a month is enough.' I notice with horror that my words are taking on the tone of a professional consultation. 'No toxic reactions . . . it's not even a poison. Just a contraceptive pill for fleas, it won't kill the bugs, just prevent their eggs hatching out.' I give a silly laugh.

At the other end of the line there's a long silence. Then I hear Angel's voice.

'Thank you.'

Then again he's silent for a long time.

'I don't understand why you're . . . telling me all this.'

'Nothing special.' It's my turn to pause. Our conversation's full of black holes that whole universes would fit into. Then I manage to say it:

'By the way, have you found out what trolls eat yet?'

Angel

When I bought a disposable syringe at the chemist's, they looked at me as if I were a heroin addict.

Leea Virtanen (ed.), *The Stolen Grandmother and Other Urban Legends*, 1987

In the Tapanila district of Helsinki, where there are one-family houses, a mother had put her baby of less than one in its pram for a sleep. She pushed the pram into the garden and kept an eye on it through the window, going out every now and then to see how the child was.

She began preparing food in the kitchen and, for a moment, forgot to keep an eye on the baby. Then the sound of her child crying came into the kitchen, but it stopped abruptly, and the mother carried on peeling potatoes. When the soup was on the stove, she went out to bring her child from the pram.

She nearly fainted when she saw there was no baby in the pram. Instead, there was an almost new-born troll youngling, wrapped up in the pram's blanket. A neighbour had seen a dark shadow slinking out of the garden. The child was never found.

Angel

Oh, this amazing anthelmintic.

Just over a week's flown by, and there haven't even been any bad side-effects from the toxic reaction. He's a whirlwind now – all energy and vigour – bright-eyed, bounding about here and there like quicksilver. He doesn't seem to be suffering from being indoors – perhaps because he's a natural cave-dweller.

Ever since Palomita fed him that catfood he's consented to eat it occasionally, but only the same brand and not always that. Fortunately, he's now consented to have quails' eggs in his diet, provided I hide them around the flat – in a large Iittala glass ashtray, or four of them making a nice little four-leaf clover-shape in a sofa cushion, or on the window-sills behind the curtains. Sometimes, when I get carried away, I make little hiding places out of gloves, cardboard boxes and coffee-pot tops and secrete them around the flat. He goes after the items, smells them, digs into them and goes into unbounded rejoicing when he finds the treasure. And then he sits down to slurp the eggs, first cracking them neatly into two halves with his fingernails and then lapping up the contents without spilling a drop.

Of course he still has a need to hunt, but I live in hope that I won't have to find any new pet shops. The ones I've been to already I can't imagine visiting for months.

Actually, his coat's not shiny yet – in fact it's looking very matted and distempered. I do hope the reason isn't the Program tablets or the anthelmintic. But I can really tell: he's healthy, healthy and happy.

Palomita

Pentti's in a hurry. Grabbing something from the bathroom, he kicks the washing basket over, and the lid rolls away with a clatter. I freeze, seeing the cover of the magazine Mikael gave me gleaming through gaps in the washing.

But he doesn't notice, he just rushes out through the door, and I sink down on the floor, my heart in my mouth. I'll have to find a new place for the magazine. I don't want to throw it away, for I've so little that's my own. Every page is a letter, every picture a little coloured doorway out of this flat.

I have a long think. I've no cupboard or drawer of my own. Though Pentti never takes a towel or sheet out of the cupboard himself, he once pulled all the things down and ordered me to put them back more neatly. Then it comes back to me how, when I was playing hiding the stone with Seppa and Miranda once, no one found the stone, because I'd taken it outside and put it with the other stones. Pentti's got hundreds of magazines piled on the floor of the clothes cupboard, and he regularly buys new ones without ever looking at the old ones. If I hide mine among them, right at the bottom, he'll surely never find it. And if he does, he may think he bought it himself. Pentti doesn't always remember everything he's done.

I go to the cupboard and start carefully lifting one of the piles out. I'm taking care to keep them in the same order. All the covers have women on. My hand falls on one that has a yellow notelet on the cover, where Pentti's written something. The cover also shows two dark-skinned women. Filipino women. They're hugging each other like sisters, but they aren't looking at each other; they're looking out of the magazine and pouting their lips. Another yellow notelet's poking out between the pages. I open there. There's a lot of print, and the pictures are totally different from the usual ones, small, some black and white and a little unclear. They all show a woman. Beside the pictures, there are words I know, and Manila comes up often.

Three of the pictures have been encircled with blue ink. In one of them there's me.

I recognize myself, though the photo's poor, and I smile though it doesn't amuse me at all. Enteng took the photo in the bar at Ermita soon after it had become clear to me I would not become a nurse.

I close the magazine and put it carefully back in its own place as I pile the rest on top of mine.

Angel

I wake in the night.

He's sitting on the sofa-back looking at me.

He's a silhouette, black as night against the slightly lighter background, and I'm seared by a tense and excruciating awareness that I'm completely at his mercy.

His eyes. The eyes of a night creature.

He sees me clearly and keenly regardless of the dark, perceives every eye-blink, every swallow of my mouth, while all I can take in are his black, black outlines.

Ecke

Odd how there can be cities and cities. Cities within cities. The dogs' city is built up of smells. For dogs, the limits of a city-block are drawn by different aromas of piss, and each smell's like a cloth fluttering in the wind or a block-long cartoon-balloon: '*Fido was here about a day and night ago.*' Or it shouts out loud: 'A YOUNGISH MALE HUMAN JUST WENT BY HERE WITH SMOKED HAM IN HIS BAG.' The air's thick with these signals, but the dog reads them as fluently and extemporaneously as a human processing the cacophony of photons from all the colours and shapes and shifts of light.

Then there are different people's cities. There's the city of a certain kind of woman, who judges a street by the kinds of shops there are, the classiness of the fashion shops, the perfumeries, jewellers, shoe-shops. An alkie's city, on the other hand, consists of pubs, sausage-stands, off-licences, alleys where you can nip in for a piss without being picked up for indecent behaviour, fellow-alkies' pads where you can scrounge the price of a drink or a bunk for the night. And he doesn't even notice the designer boutique because it's got no function for him, just as the fashionable lady doesn't see that sleazy pub – it doesn't exist for her. She knows a certain street corner well because of a coffee-shop she some-times drops into, for a cappuccino and a fancy cake. The bus-driver's city is a mass of routes, stops, traffic-lights, hills and of corners that look completely insignificant, except that their magic lies in their trickiness under certain winter conditions. There are terminuses every inch of which are familiar and meaningful because he's loafed about there, fag in mouth, waiting for his time to go back. He even knows every squirrel in the trees, too, though the casual passer-by sees nothing but a bit of broader road worn down by heavy wheels.

Our city's unique, but with a slightly different nuance for each of us. In a little town like this, we don't have our own streets, shops or gal-leries, but we do have our individual hidden topography, our own street corners. A man's pulling on a fag at the corner of a bridge, and we see him quite differently to everyone else: we take in a hand movement, an eye-glance, which, for others, are just visual bric-à-brac. We know holes and corners and lanes and gateways that have a significance entirely their own. There are car parks and certain film-shows, perfectly unremarkable to the rest of the community but charged with invisible magnetism for us. There are public lavatories you go to with more excited expectations than some other punter going on a blind date. And then there are boozers like this Café Bongo, where every Tom, Dick or Harriet can drop in for a pint, put two or three away, or get completely pissed and leave as if it were any other faceless corner bar, not noticing anything special. Our radar alone picks up the out-of-sight idiosyncrasies.

The atmosphere in the Café Bongo is perpetually criss-crossed by so many silent messages that, were they visible, the whole dive would be rainbow-coloured spiders' webs from floor to ceiling: red strands of lust, blue longings, waitings and hopings, tingling yellow signals that it's time to take the first step – permission's been covertly asked and covertly granted – and, naturally, there has also to be some coal-black thread of contempt and disappointment and outright hatred.

There are the moments when certain figures set themselves up to be taken. As the evening advances, they leave their companions' tables and make a momentary window-display. But only for those who see.

It's as if most people had a layer of clingfilm over their senses. It doesn't stop them seeing, so they think they're noticing everything; but the clingfilm stops the operation of certain other senses. And they don't even notice how it muffles those brushes, touchings and scents.

Like that breeder-woman sitting at the bar, who thinks it's a buzz to go into a gay joint and has no doubt heard somewhere that this is one. Her lurid get-up's a joke, ludicrous. She's the type who dons camouflage-green combat trousers, wraps a bandanna around her head and paints herself with black lipstick, imagining all the lesbians in the joint'll have the hots for her. Not so much imagining as secretly hoping.

Naturally, no one goes and sits with her. She's been here before, and everyone gives her the ice-cold shoulder, yet still she turns up again and again. Someone might argue we're zoo animals for her. But I've another theory. For her, we're noble savages, a kind of grey area outside the respectable, minutely organized community, an untamed wilderness it takes a lot of guts to step into. But if you do dare, there's a glorious smell of freedom floating around your trousers and giving the finger to society, making whoever an instant anarchist. Certainly, for her, coming here is like putting a washable tattoo on your shoulder: there's the thrill of deviance with none of the dull commitment – and she'll never have to wonder whether she's too weird to be seen out before dark.

Barton Willman, *The Black And The Invisible:*
A Fantasy Romance, **1985**

It is said – it was a wise man from the far North who told me – it is said that, in certain parts of Scandinavia, there are cities within cities, just as there are circles within circles, existent yet invisible. And those cities are inhabited by creatures more terrible than imagination can create: man-shaped but man-devouring, as black and silent as the night they prowl in.

Angel

I tip the lettered building blocks out under the lights and go to the viewfinder to check the shadows are falling correctly. I arrange the bricks to form the name of my client firm, set them up nicely at impressive angles and begin to photograph a series, building up the enterprise's name from the bricks, letter by letter. I start with the whole word, of course, and then reduce the bricks one by one, as then it's easier for me to control the shadows, and I don't have to shift well-placed pieces around. I take my Polaroid, and it looks good.

The work's sheer routine, and so I've left the door between my studio and the flat open. It's eight o'clock at night, and I can hear that Pessi's woken up and is eating his first meal.

I take all the photos, it's peanuts, a bread-and-butter job not to be compared with Martes' project. I switch the studio lights off, gather up the building blocks and chuck them in their boxes. The firm's daft name has so many of the same letters in it I needed two boxes. Pity I can't return them, but the cellophane wrapping's all torn. Well, the client'll have that little extra on his bill as well.

I go into my pad and open a beer, sit in an armchair and flick the television on. Soon Pessi comes to pester me to do things. He plays just like a cat, trying to catch any old object, for as long as I can be bothered to wave it about.

The news begins, and I'm idly dangling his toy about during the first headlines – the exchange news, crisis in Pakistan, a Parola arms depot's been broken into, quite a haul of firearms, doubtless stolen by the Russian mafia . . . But the next item makes me sit up and forget the little game with Pessi.

'Possibly because of the mildness of the early winter, the large animals that would normally be hibernating are still very active.

'In the late autumn there were many sightings of bears and trolls near the eastern frontier, but now the sightings have increased in the interior of Finland as well. In the rural commune of Jyväskylä, as many as three sightings of trolls are alleged to have taken place during the last week. That equals the whole count during the last forty years. These large animals habitually withdraw and hibernate during November at the latest, but now traces of them have frequently been encountered at favoured summer-cottage sites on the shores of Lake Päijänne and elsewhere. In addition, there have been almost certain sightings of trolls as far south as Heinola, Janakkala and Pälkäne, in the neighbourhood of Tampere.'

They interview a granny who's seen strange things on the path to her shed, and then some Oulu game-researcher called Ilpo Kojola appears on the screen. He emphasizes that the troll is in principle unadapted to winter activity, but he adds that in mild winters bears too may withdraw to their dens much later than usual. He points out that if the trolls have not accumulated enough food reserves in the autumn they may now be hastily trying to supplement their supplies before constructing their dens and have thus moved from their normal hunting grounds and closer to towns.

An opposing view is presented by an environmentalist, who doubts the food-shortage story but reminds us that poisoning of the environment may cause exceptional behaviour in animals. 'Fledgelings and birds' nests form a significant part of the troll's diet in many areas, and, notoriously, all residues in the environment find their way into birds' eggs. It's conceivable that because of the fire at the Karasjoki transformer in Lapland, for example, trolls which have eaten birds' eggs may have their systems saturated with tetrachloride dibenzoic-p-dioxin.'

The interviewer's just asking what the effect of tetrachloride whatchermecallit might be, and the environmentalist is beginning to speak about mutations, when I realize that Pessi is suspiciously quiet and he must be up to mischief. I look around for him. He's sitting crouched up as always, his thin black back and brush towards me, his ears trembling as they register the noises around, and his tail swaying as a sign of extreme concentration. I get up from my chair, and now I see, even though the room's almost dark, that Pessi has taken the building blocks and, with his prehensile long-nailed fingers, is at this very moment putting one on the summit of an almost faultless pyramid.

Harto Lindén, 'The Effects of Hunting on the Game Stock',
Hunting – Nature – Society, **Petri Nummi (ed.), 1995**

To some degree, large size always threatens the future of an animal breed. The stock of the large breeds is on the whole small, making accidental factors, perhaps associated with splitting up of stock, drive a breed into a cycle of attenuation. The large-sized breeds are endangered by any increase, for whatever reason, in the mortality of mature animals. At present, the large animals, with their small populations, are experiencing genetic difficulties in a rapidly changing environment. Their size is adapted to a predictable and/or unchanging environment; the current environmental instability, therefore, constitutes a serious threat to them. An allied consideration is that a weakening in the quality of the environment can often diminish a large animal's opportunities for daily nourishment.

The increase in mature mortality can be too small-scale easily to facilitate scientific measurement. The effect can nevertheless be dramatic.

Angel

Again and again Pessi takes the top bricks off the pyramid and replaces them in slightly different positions. I hear an extremely low, almost inaudible sound. He's purring. He's enjoying himself.

My mouth's dry as dust. Something in the shape of the pyramid bothers me, some memory teases me. I take a couple of quick strides over to the bookshelf. The books my brother left are all together in a corner of the bookshelf, tucked away almost out of sight behind various new and second-hand books about beasts of prey that I've picked up. There are about ten books of his, hardly glanced at, but I haven't been able to bring myself to get rid of them.

That's it. Eero Ojanen's *Prehistoric Remains in Finland*. I turn to the list of illustrations, and there it is: a cairn, a pyramid of cobblestones. 'The crowned territorial marker at Salo,' the caption says, but I know what it is all right, regardless of the misleading nomenclature.

A devil's stove.

Of Finland's three thousand devil's stoves, most have been proved to be bronze-age cremation sites, but there are also piles of cobblestones the function of which is not exactly known, 'Lapp ruins' and 'giants' churches'. According to one study they were territorial markers, and the cairn of stones was their 'crown'.

They're also referred to as 'racketstoves' or noisy stoves, and some folk tales relate that the ancient woods were inhabited by a 'noisy race'. According to these stories the goblins or other woodsprites played about on the racketstoves, and that's why weird sounds came from there.

The Lapp ruins may also be places of sacrifice, because the bones of game animals are often found both in and around them.

The shape of the cairns and the caches of bones also suggest some Lapland stone idols, which were in ancient times considered the idols of a creature called the *staalo*.

Animal bones?

Tell me, books. On the cairns and in their surroundings were there bones of reindeer, elk, fox, wolverine? Wolf bones, bear bones, the slender skeletons of lynxes?

Or did the archaeologists – tell me, books, and you don't tell – happen on surprising numbers of bones from those animals whose carcasses are otherwise so rarely encountered in the wild . . . troll bones?

Anni Swan, *The Mountain Troll and the Shepherd Girl*, 1933

The whole mountain shook and boomed, boulders rumbled down, and the girl only just managed to jump out of the cave mouth before the whole gorge sank thundering into a heap of rocks, and nothing was left of the mountain troll's handsome halls but grey boulders and moss.

The mountain troll no one has heard of or seen since. Has he perhaps been buried there under the stones of his cave? But the shepherd girl hurried off back home, to her green forest, her pastures and the shore of the blue sea.

Part 3

Who Cares If Brightness Makes Me Blind

Angel

Pessi's coat is moulting in tufts, so my whole pad is a mass of coal-black balls of fluff, and all the chair-covers and curtains and carpets are greyish with hair. I try to vacuum it clean and, while the vacuum's going, Pessi invariably does a lightning dash to the coat-rack, crawls up my trench-coat sleeve, ripping it to shreds, and squats demonstratively above, the very image of a saturnine gargoyle on a Notre Dame wall. He hates the noise of the vacuum, though luckily he's gradually getting a little used to it.

He doesn't seem ill at all, though the shreds of his coat are a dismal sight in the Electrolux.

I phone the duty vet under an assumed name and describe Pessi's moulting. I say it's a dog and enquire if the recently administered parasite medicine might be partially to blame. The vet says no, it shouldn't have that sort of effect, and asks the breed. My fib is that he's a mongrel with a lot of husky in him.

'He's otherwise completely playful and normal.'

The vet reflects a moment.

'It would sound like a quite normal shedding of a winter coat, if this were the late spring, but . . .'

I breathe deeply. Shedding a winter coat. Naturally.

Normally at this time of year a troll would be deep asleep under the snow, in a hole in the rock, or, exceptionally, he'd be shivering on the outskirts of Kuopio, still in his thick coat, scaring the locals. But my warm flat, an even twenty degrees centigrade, is a new springtime for Pessi, a spring ahead of schedule.

The vet recommends bringing the dog to the clinic, and I eagerly promise to ring as soon as I've checked my diary. Pessi's asleep on the sofa, and my heart's so full of joy and relief that I go to plant a kiss between his pointy ears as they tremble in sleep.

Palomita

It's so dark.

We have a proverb: in the house the man's the mainstay, his wife a light.

They told me it meant you can manage without a light, but without a mainstay everything tumbles down.

In the morning when Pentti wakes up it's dark. When he comes from work it's dark. In the middle of the day there's a small grey moment.

Here we get along with no light. Without a wife. For I am no wife, even though I'm married. I'm a concubine, *querida*. What man wants a wife but no children?

When I came here and Pentti still only scared me a little, he took me to the doctor and spoke right past me. I knew he was saying I couldn't understand what they were talking about, because the doctor never asked me anything, only Pentti, and I was put on to a sort of rack, where the doctor looked at me and felt me, so tears came into my eyes, and then he pushed something in me that Pentti told me later would stop me having children.

I wept because I'd done so great a sin. I wept for days and only stopped when I got a punishment for it, but now I'm not so very sad any more. Not about that, though it must be a small sin, at least, even to think that way. There are places where it's not good for children to be.

Here it's so cold.

Angel

He wakes up in the evening and climbs on to the window-sill to see the Christmas lights glowing in Pirkankatu Street. He seeks out the quails' eggs I've hidden, and when he finds them bounces about like a colt let out to pasture. He jumps on to the sofa and sits beside me as I watch the TV, so that his juniper smell drifts into my nostrils like a waft of perfume.

The short fur now showing from under his former long sleek coat is so exiguous, so tight to his skin, it's almost as though it weren't fur at all but a glossy black cuticle. The mane around his head has not moulted, though, and so Pessi's slim two-legged form, seen from a distance, resembles quite confusingly a slightly stylized boy, human-looking, like some of the animal stars in children's cartoon films. His small firm muscles function with extreme precision and contained energy.

His movements have an unselfconscious seductiveness.

For minutes on end, with his head on one side, he follows the movements of my hand as I operate the mouse of my computer.

I'm churning over and on fire.

'Calvin Klein Stimulates Ocelots', *Finnish Morning Post* (5 August 1999); Reuters, Dallas

Researchers at the Dallas Zoological Gardens have made a promising discovery in their attempts to encourage ocelots to multiply. A smell that stimulates the males of this rare breed of the cat family has at last been discovered – and it appears to be Calvin Klein's eau-de-Cologne, Obsession for Men.

Four caged ocelot females reacted more strongly to the Klein than to natural aromas being tested with the aim of encouraging ocelots to breed in the wild, says zoo researcher Dr Cynthia Bennett.

'Among other substances, we experimented with rat excrement and the ocelots' own aromas. Then an assistant produced the Cologne, because many animals appreciate it, and the smell drove the ocelots wild,' Bennett said.

This feline breed began to roll and writhe on the spots where the Cologne had been sprinkled. The reaction resembled displays of affection by domestic cats.

In the wild, there are only about 100–120 individuals of this Texas sub-species of the ocelot, and undirected by smells the animals have difficulty in locating one other.

Angel

Just now I want something so badly it hurts, and so I don't care whom I harm or how much.

Ecke

Angel's so gorgeous it makes me ache. It's as if a Finland-Film stud – a lumberjack, balanced on a log in his turned-up boots – were manoeuvring the log-jam away with his boat-hook, his curly fair forelock flopping over his stern eyes and his upper torso shining with sweat. I slip into the seat beside him and put my mug on the table. Angel gives a sideways glance but no glimmer of interest.

'I'm Ecke. And they call you Angel. As a matter of fact, I'm not a bit surprised.'

Angel's lip curls. 'My real name's Mikael.'

I pretend I've only just realized. 'Oh that's where it comes from, of course. The Archangel.'

Angel looks as if he's heard that before, but I charge ahead on my chosen path.

'So, of course, you must know that you're the patron of Sunday. According to the astrologers, each day has its angel: Saturday Cassiel, Sunday Mikael, Monday Gabriel, Tuesday Camael, Wednesday Raphael, Thursday Sachiel.'

'That's inconceivably interesting,' Angel states in a voice full of sarcasm, but at the same time I can see he's falling into the trap. 'Especially since you forgot Friday.'

'I'm not a bit surprised you want to know *that*. Friday's angel is, of course, dear old Anael.'

Angel almost spits a mouthful of ale on to the table. 'You made that up.'

I smile with the maximum of ambiguity. 'Actually, different books give slightly different accounts. You can come up and consult my source books whenever you fancy it.'

Angel laughs again, and his look shows that I now exist for him, and I congratulate myself quickly: Ecke, you've done it again.

Jukka Koskimies, 'Hierarchy in the Animal World', *Science for the Young*, 5, 1965

In the world of aquarium fish, in the nesting communities and wintering flocks of wild birds, as well as in the communities of rats, dogs, wolves, trolls, many kinds of elks, apes and – of course – human beings, certain individuals have a strong aspiration to dominate, while others prefer to serve.

What then is the foundation of such a hierarchical principle in the animal kingdom? Apparently, each individual obtains his status in the community on the basis of some first impression. When two individuals meet it appears instantly clear which is the dominant one and which the subservient. Nor, in general, are any physical clashes necessary. The one who makes the more powerful and competent impression, from its external appearance and above all the confidence of its behaviour, will see submission in the other. And the relationship thus established endures for a very long time, unchanged, until, some day perhaps, for whatever reason, it is reconsidered. In this way each individual makes clear its relationship to every other individual, and the end result is soon settled and – what is more astonishing – understood by all. Unerringly, each individual assesses every other member of the group and knows how to relate to it.

Ecke

Angel's flank next to mine is like a furnace. We're in that when-the-sweat's-already-dried state, when it's toughest of all to find something to say.

Earlier in the evening it was easier. Angel nattered away about his childhood in the north, his adolescence, and after the third pint he mentioned his kid brother – two years younger than himself, an archaeologist and an extremely gifted devotee of nature photography. His brother died a year ago. A stray shot in the forest, and it wasn't even the elk-hunting season. He was missing for several weeks, and then someone out berrying stumbled on the body. Bullet-hole in the neck. No one knows who fired it, and the bullet wasn't ever found. I remember putting my hand on his hand and squeezing it unabashedly and Angel raising his eyes to mine, and at that point my heart started to dance the cha-cha-cha.

Angel's lying on his stomach, and I run my hand along his back and his behind.

He gives the faintest of shivers, and then it goes just as I've feared. With a careless, oh-how-artificially-casual-seeming movement, as if on the spur of the moment, he's sitting up, groping for his jeans and sweeping the blond quiff from his forehead, and my pulse goes off at a gallop, because his lips are just about to formulate the sentence I don't want to hear.

Angel

Ecke is small and dark, what you might call nerdy. Bad haircut, thick glasses, and he's narrow-shouldered, short-legged, with a rather wide bottom. Not at all my type.

His flat's encrusted with books. They grow up the walls, proliferating over everything like a polychromatic invasion of moss. They aspire to places outside their own reserve, they push four-cornered tentacles on to window-sills, tables, chairs and the floor. You can't take a step without tripping over a book. Even the hall, the lavatory and the rather diminutive bedroom are lined with books. The paperbacks stand two rows deep on the shelves. In the midst of this jungle of books, however, there looms the monitor of Ecke's computer. Ecke's a PC man and I've a Macintosh, and in the course of the evening we moved on to comparing their respective merits. It turned into a hilarious mad wrangle. I told all my Bill Gates jokes, claimed Microsoft had lifted all its best ideas from Apple, and finally we went into a hugely rewarding nitpicking. I threw in that people had to wait until Windows 98 for the chance to have several monitors on the same machine, whereas for years Mac had been providing this absolutely indispensable facility for creatives like me. The whole session was half-rumpus, half-flirtation, a love song composed of gags and disparaging cracks, the sort of thing I had some years ago with an absolutely irresistible photographer boy about the respective merits of Nikon and Canon.

I wander into Ecke's living-room, stroll around and examine the backs of the books. I ought to go, but I can't. I'm not finding the right words to shake Ecke's hot-glue look off the back of my neck.

Pessi's never been alone for a whole night before.

'It's not all that tidy here,' Ecke goes on when I run my finger along the bindings and loosen a quantity of dust. 'But I *have* tried, a bit, to keep some sort of order, because I once had a really traumatic experience . . .'

I smirk a little and stand looking at a glass case with some really old books in. Ecke runs a combination second-hand book and computer-component shop, but, from what he says, most of the books finally end up in his own home. The young computer freaks only go for the odd comic book.

'I was living in Pispala at that time, in the stone basement of somebody's house. A poor student's cheap bedsit. Wood-burning stove and all. No proper storage space, just a couple of ridiculous cupboards. Nowhere decent for coffee mugs, glasses and so on. And then I came across a couple of bits of chipboard in the shed, and with those and a few bricks I knocked together a sort of a shelf-extension to the zinc washing-up board.'

I open the glass case carefully. The books give off an overpowering smell of old paper – the smell's somewhat like an outdoor wood-saw after rain – and it's a good special effect in Ecke's story.

'Came summer, a long hot summer, and those chipboards by the sink must have had piles of soakings during the washings-up. One morning I'd been spending too long in a beer garden the night before, and I got up with a bit of a hangover, went into the kitchen for a drink of water and simply let out a yell.'

Tickled, I turn and look at Ecke. He's raising his hands, a sheepish look on his face.

'The chipboard's growing mushrooms about six inches high. Pale violet-grey and revolting. Broad caps, gills, the lot.'

I give a snort of incredulous laughter.

'Mushrooms. On your washing-up board.'

'Mushrooms. A . . . a type who was there with me at the time lewdly suggested I rustle them up into a mushroom omelette for breakfast. But, retching away, I chucked out the whole chipboard contraption. Underneath it had become pure compost.'

I pull a face. 'Straight out of a surrealist film.'

'Peter Greenaway, of course. New masterpiece: *Nature Strikes Back*. A tale of the wild wood stealthily insinuating itself into the hygienic life of urban dwellers who suspect no evil. Scene Two: a mother's tampon box grows a fir-tree cone.'

My laugh's a bit false as I turn to examine the books again. Straight away, my fingers light on an antiquated-looking volume, and I pull it out.

I take a deep breath.

Gustaf Eurén: *The Wild Beasts of Finland, Illustrated in Colour.*

'That's from 1854,' Ecke says. He's suddenly behind me.

I turn to him: 'Lend me this.'

Ecke

Angel looks shockingly beautiful standing there with the Eurén book in his hand, so beautiful my hand pauses, my hand that was just about to go to his shoulders and draw him down towards me, with his blond shock of hair. He's pressing the Gustaf Eurén, a rare antiquarian piece, a pearl of great price, against his naked chest.

'It's terribly old. And terribly expensive.' I can't help feeling how sordid I'm sounding. Suddenly I'm a miserly, penny-pinching old skin-flint hanging on to his merchandise, who can't let a single dusty item slip through his claws.

'I'd really like to read this, an awful lot.'

I look at Angel desperately. I can see from the look in his eye how he's weighing me up. How far am I willing to go because he's gifted and successful and beautiful and hellishly sexy, and as far above me as a free-running lynx above a soon-to-be-skinned mink crouching in its cage with no weapons but its slipperiness and small but sharp teeth.

'And I'd really like an awful lot for nothing to happen to this. There are very few of them around in Finland.'

'Well, bound to be so.'

'I don't normally lend my books. But, well, here, at my place . . . you can read them as much as you like.'

I know at once how it sounds. *Why not come into my lair, young man?* Come, and let me entangle you in my web, so you'll never find your way out again.

Angel has a very serious look. He thrusts the Eurén towards me like a goodbye letter.

'Okay. No, then. I understand. This must be a thing you really value.'

And his tone of voice throws down the glove: if this book's valuable, then how valuable am *I* then?

'You'd not believe its list price.'

Angel turns, sighs and pretends to put the book back in the case. And I know just as well as he does that it's an act, that he's giving me an opportunity. And I pick up the cue: I seize Angel's wrist – the golden swell of those wrist bones, that finely dewed skin – and stop him.

'Take it.'

Angel's laugh has a low note of triumph in it. He slides the hands holding the book around my back and kisses me on the lips quickly and hard. A bony kiss, I think. A bone to a good dog. And his eyes glow.

'And don't go using a slice of salami as a bookmark' is my parting shot, and Angel smirks with just the right delight, just the right casualness, to show me my Angelic visitation's over, the magical moment has passed, and what's left is just a cramp in my stomach and a floorful of rubber relics of joy.

Angel

I'm sitting in a chair in my bathrobe, and I open the book. I've just had my evening shower, and I'm waiting for Pessi to finish his breakfast before I clean the bathroom.

'The number of wild animals in Finland is very large, and all of these beasts are destructive,' Eurén begins. He scrupulously records the animals' distinguishing characteristics and physical structure. I hear thumpings from the bathroom and nails scratching the floor. Pessi's hunting a panting guinea-pig around the floor-tiles and hurling the creature at the walls from time to time; so once again I'll have to spend quite some time cleaning the splatterings off with Ocean Fresh Flash.

> And since different weapons are needed for the mastication of different substances, the shape of the teeth alone may well enable us to determine what each animal's sustenance is. Again, the pabulum helps us to determine the means of motion each particular animal will need for obtaining the particular nourishment its teeth are adapted to, and also the strength and other physical characteristics required for winning each kind of food, carrying it, and so forth; and thus we may almost always, simply from the teeth, determine the configuration of the whole animal.

I hear a squeak and crunch, because I've been too late in gauging when to put my hands over my ears. Pessi has crunched through the guinea-pig's backbone. Appropriately, Eurén is just coming to the cat family.

> The largest creatures of this family are formidable predators. Such are the lion, the tiger, the leopard and the lynx. Hunters also have tales of, on occasion, sighting a troll or forest demon and also the creature called, because of its nimbleness, the thicket demon, an animal which many of them consider a species of cat or large ape. Nevertheless, those who claim to have seen troll-type creatures are extremely rare, even more so those who might have obtained them as booty; so we may

be permitted to consider the 'forest demon' as pure fabrication and fancy.

I take my hands cautiously off my ears. It's quiet. Evidently Pessi's now eating. Eurén continues about cats.

These animals also resemble snakes in their mottled or spotted appearance, the slyness of their nature, the circularity of their reclining posture and the foul stench they emit when enraged.

I grin. The door creaks and Pessi comes out of the bathroom, looking at peace and satisfied, his small red tongue licking around his mouth like a flame. He bounces straight on to my lap on the sofa and wraps himself into a ball on my knees. His juniper-berry smell pungently overpowers my nostrils, and on my thighs his warm weight, glowing with the excitement of the hunt, is a burden. He's lazily cleaning the blood from the corners of his mouth, when, hardly knowing what I'm doing, I draw him a little closer to me, just a little and ever so cautiously – and the moment his hot back touches my belly I ejaculate like a volcano.

My heart's hammering and thumping, like a rock-drill. The sperm has spattered Pessi's back and my thighs, and I'm doing my level best not to think about what's just happened. I've instinctively put the faded fragile book aside, and Pessi's just moving away a little, not provoked but to make himself more comfortable, for he's in the process of cleaning himself, and I thrust him out of my lap – so abruptly, violently almost, that he takes fright, bolts into the hall and tries to scramble up on to the hat-rack. His powerful, clambering hind legs hit the hall mirror, and the heavy frame bangs down on the thick carpet, while I'm dashing into the bathroom to wash away my shameful stain.

Ancient Poems of the Finnish People, **VII. 1. 375, 1929,**
'The Marriage Proposal to the Trolls', collected from
Trofim Sosonov, the village of Uomaa, Impilahti

'What do folk then call you men?'
'Fishermen with seines be we.'
'Where to do you fare for brides?'
'Fare we to the Devil's daughters,
Children of the mountain tribes.'

Angel

I don't want to do what I'm doing, but I must.

I'm putting Pessi in a child's pushchair I've borrowed from the stairwell: no one'll be needing it, now it's night. I've wrapped him up in a travelling rug so that no one coming along will start wondering. Pessi's ears stir, and his nostrils are trembling at the mass of city smells.

Below Pyynikki ridge, on the outskirts of the forest leading to Pirkkala, I peel the travelling rug off him. I take off his collar and lead, which I've been using to fasten him to the pushchair. He crouches in the chair, black and naked and trembling, while a single snowflake flutters down on to his black mane and soon melts into a tear.

'Go,' I whisper. 'Go.'

Pessi's shivering gets worse. My hands feel his trembling as I lift him to stand up in the snow. I point the pushchair the other way and set off for the town again, trying not to look back.

My footsteps on the path creak comfortlessly. Suddenly they're joined by another sound, a furious scratching of nails, and before I can even turn something hits my right thigh like a tiger.

Pessi's clinging on to my leg with all four limbs and looking up, straight into my face, so intensely it's like a blow. He lets a little mewing sound out of his throat. He's trembling so violently it makes me sway.

He'll not get by in the winter. He's naked, and I've made him naked.

Mikael Agricola, Preface to
The Finnish Translation of the Psalms, 1551

Victims to the trolls were led,
Widows did they take and wed.
Are the people not gone mad,
Trusting trolls, a tribe gone bad.
Steered by Satan to sinful stem,
They worship trolls and pray to them.

Angel

The mirror's lying on the hall carpet. I'm not lifting it. I'm just crouched there beside it, panting. I can't function, can't coordinate.

The travelling rug's back on the sofa. Pessi's still trembling a little, but clearly he's beginning to calm down. He's resting his back against the radiator, his tail twitching very slightly like the needle of some delicate instrument.

And then he comes into the hall, cautiously, wondering at my immobility and my bowed head. The mirror's a small round pond in the fluffy carpet.

I lean over the mirror, and my face is reflected there. Next to my own, a smaller, dark face appears, with pointed ears, a twinkle of curiosity in its orange eyes.

Pessi tests the mirror with his paw. He looks at me and then back at the reflection. He shows his teeth but recoils a little when the troll in the mirror returns his grimace; but then he edges back to the mirror and again tests the cold glass surface with his paw.

We look at each other, me and the troll. The lamplight's casting a pale halo around my head, and at my side Pessi is a dark silhouette. We look at each other and then at the mirror and then back at each other.

Päivänsäde Ja Menninkäinen
('Goldwing and Troll'; words and music, Reino Helismaa, 1949)

Aurinko kun päätti retken, siskoistaan jäi jälkeen hetken
    Päivänsäde viimeinen.
Hämärä jo metsään hiipi; Päivänsäde kultasiipi
    juuri aikoi lentää eestä sen,
kun Menninkäisen pienen näki vastaan tulevan;
    se juuri oli noussut luolostaan.
Kas: Menninkäinen ennen päivän laskua ei voi
    milloinkaan olla päällä maan.

Katselivat toisiansa. Menninkäinen rinnassansa
    tunsi kuumaa leiskuntaa.
Sanoi: 'Poltat silmiäni, mutt' en ole eläissäni
    nähnyt mitään yhtä ihanaa!
Ei haittaa, vaikka loisteesi mut sokeaksi saa:
    on pimeässä hyvä asustaa.
Käy kanssani, niin kotiluolaan näytän sulle tien,
    ja sinut armaakseni vien.'

Säde vastas: 'Peikko kulta, pimeys vie hengen multa,
    enkä toivo kuolemaa.
Pois mun täytyy heti mennä: ellen kohta valoon lennä,
    niin en hetkeäkään elää saa!'
Niin lähti kaunis Päivänsäde, mutta vieläkin,
    kun Menninkäinen öisin tallustaa,
hän miettii: 'Miksi toinen täällä valon lapsi on,
    ja toinen yötä rakastaa?'

Goldwing and Troll

When the sun had done his run, one sister sunray,
    Goldwing, lingered on.
Dusk crept through the greenwood. Goldwing
    flared her wings to flee away,
when up woke Troll and came to meet her –
    creeping from his hidden cave:
not before sundown dare he greet the
    earth from out his daytime grave.

She stared, and he stared. In his heart there flared
    a wondrous glow of light.
'You burn my eyes,' he said, 'and yet you bless:
    I've never seen such loveliness!
Who cares if brightness makes me blind?
    Dark to me is always kind.
Come see my cave, my wildwood life,
    and live with me and be my wife.'

But Goldwing said: 'O darling Troll, darkness takes my
    soul away. I'll die.
I must wing my way to day at once – must fly
    to light, or fade, grow chill.'
So his gorgeous Goldwing left, but still when Troll
    goes plodding on through night
he thinks and thinks: 'Why is one the child of light,
    while the other loves the night?'

Angel

Martti's vanished from my mind completely. Seems inconceivable. But, now, hearing his voice on the phone turns my legs to jelly.

His voice is soft and a bit husky as always, but I don't want to believe his words, not those words.

He's wondering why I haven't reported how I'm getting on with the Stalker project. Or am I really spending all my time running after some horse-doctor in the Tampere city night, as the whole town seems to know?

I try to blurt out an explanation: there's still time before the deadline, I've certainly come up with ideas, but just now there's been a tiny bottleneck . . . But a poisonous sarcasm is drizzling into Martes' words: obviously I'm not approaching his brief with the slightest seriousness, obviously I'm not taking this whole cooperative enterprise of ours seriously enough. The Stalker campaign's crucial for him, one of the biggest challenges of his career. I'm not thinking of letting him down, am I . . . in this, too?

I hear everything that's hidden between the lines.

There are tears in my eyes as the phone clicks down.

Excerpt from the Schools' Television Programme
Is a Predatory Animal Cruel? (19 October 1999)

Professor Martti Soikkeli of Turku University reports: 'Cruelty is knowingly – consciously – causing another being mental or physical pain, agony, and doing it regardless of the knowledge that the other is suffering anguish. So now, asked if predatory animals kill and rend their prey with the knowledge they are causing pain and agony, then the answer is categorically no: they do not know. In the animal kingdom there is no such thing as what is called morality – in other words, knowledge of good and evil. We human beings are moral beings: we know the difference between good and evil; but animals do not.'

Angel

In the studio I take Pessi in my arms then whisk the Stalkers on to his back legs with a single pull – knowing I'd not manage it at a second shot. If Pessi had thought of spreading his hind claws, the jeans wouldn't have slipped on: the legs would have been torn to shreds. A size to fit a three-foot-six-inch child suits him stunningly. I've got the zip and metal button fastened and have twitched his tail through the hole I've made in the Stalker backside before he realizes he's been diddled. Then I throw Pessi – now a hissing, whirling ball bristling with razor-sharp claws – in front of the backdrop, and I start the automatic camera rolling.

Pessi hates the Stalkers – so fiercely he doesn't take a jump at the walls but stays put, right there where he should be, against the backdrop, illuminated by the lamps, in my viewfinder. He's somersaulting, pirouetting, doing his damnedest to get rid of this indigo-blue straitjacket imprisoning his back legs. The lights must be causing his night-vision eyes intense pain, but it's the struggle with the Stalkers that takes priority in Pessi's mind. He leaps a metre high with his amazing springs of muscles, twists and turns like a grotesque boy go-go dancer, does a break-dance roll on his back and tries to rip the jeans with his foreclaws. But the denim's holding, it's holding for the time being, and Pessi stretches upright, stands on his two legs, nails ripping at the belt loops, and I almost shut my eyes – it's such a perfect frame. Then he presses his black mane into the backdrop's white floor, raises his backside, crowned of course with an impotently flourishing frenzied tail, and screams through his legs at the camera. And the shutter's whirring. And a tightly coiled coal-black and indigo-blue spring is hissing and wriggling and hurtling and jerking and circling and squirming, and it's all being shot, two frames a second, almost as if Pessi's own scintillating energy was blazing the shots on to the silver.

When the denim does finally rip, it's a relief for me, too. When the first rent comes at the hip, where Pessi can reach most easily with his claws, it's as if I'm drawing my first breath in aeons. And after that I see a whirlwind of indigo denim-shreds, with Pessi panting in the middle and then springing with a single leap out of the glare of the spotlights.

He leaps at me with a snarl, his eyes burning, his nails bared, but when I raise my hand he remembers the threat, remembers the rolled-up newspaper and dashes into a corner to curl up. I reel the diapositive on to its cassette, drop it in my hand and squeeze it. And there in the dark corner I can make out Pessi's tail, switching, switching and lashing like an angry whip.

Troll Tales, edited by the Finnish Literature Society, 1990, told by Roope Hollman, a hired hand from the village of Haukivuori, 1884

Once some foemen came to a house in the evening, claiming to be travelling men, and asked a lodging for the night. But the man of the house said, 'So few sheds we have here, we can give thee no lodging for the night. By the wood, though, we have an outhouse. If that will serve thy turn, then lay thee down there for the night.'

The foemen went to the outhouse. But, lo and behold, the morning brought a troll that had set up home in the outhouse. The troll began to ransack the foemen's backpacks and stuff the meat it found there in its mouth. When the foemen woke to this, they began to shout to the farmer, 'Hey, man, call off this black tufted-tailed cat of thine!' The farmer made as if he didn't hear the foemen's jabbering and just lay there, at his rest. Again a foeman bellowed, 'Hey, thee there, an end to this tufted-tailed cat of thine, or I'll do the thing myself!'

The farmer said not a word. Two or three more times the foeman bellowed 'An end to it, an end to it!' and then made to seize the troll. But the troll was no ordinary cat, and in two shakes of its tail the foemen had taken to their heels through the window and away in the field.

Seven years later came a foeman again to the same village. He asked the children at the field-end, 'Hast thou still that black tufted-tailed cat here with thee?'

'Yes,' the children said. 'That we do!'

At that the foeman never dared return to the house again.

Martes

I look at the screen again, zoom closer and find myself taking a deep breath. 'Fucking brilliant,' I mouth to myself, silently and with emphasis. God, it was worth it, it was worth it.

Mikael's beaming away somewhere behind my back, so close I feel the glowing warmth of his thighs, and it makes me uncomfortable. I swing around on my revolving chair, perhaps too swiftly.

'You did this with Photoshop?'

'That's right.'

I shake my head, smile against my will and see my smile's instantly reflected on Mikael's face – I've flicked it on as if with a switch.

'You're an actual wizard. Not a wipe or intercut in sight anywhere, even when I'm looking for them. Well, maybe where you've linked the tail to the trousers there's a faint blur, but you'd certainly need my professional sparrow-hawk's eye to spot that.'

Mikael grimaces, embarrassed.

'Mind you, we've seen this sort of stuff before. Take a bunch of good animal pics, then get a model with jeans on to take up the same postures as the beast, scan the stuff, and bob's your uncle. Or what? Bloody massive job you've done, anyway.'

'Didn't take so very long.'

'Always the modest violet. And the troll pictures – from the Ähtäri Animal Park archives or what?'

Mikael laughs nervously. He knows the joke, and it's an old one. In the office whenever we have an ad idea with any sort of animal in it – a bear, a mole, a penguin, or whatever – and someone starts headaching about where we'll get the rushes, someone else always says 'from the Ähtäri Animal Park archives', even if what we're looking for is a white rhinoceros.

'There won't be any trouble over the rights for these pictures, will there? Presumably you scanned the source pictures from some international nature-picture archive . . . You can't have done these takes crouching in some hide near a reindeer carcass. Where did you download them?'

Mikael explains he's got a brother whose job is photographing nature pictures for a photographic agency. He took a trip to the Russian Karelian area, where trolls are more numerous. There some local Russki found the troll in an illegal bear trap he'd set, and Mikael's brother turned up before the animal was finished off. That does explain the frames' astonishing focus, the impression of close-ups and the fact that there's no undergrowth or anything. Otherwise Mikael has cleaned up and intensified the pictures so masterfully you'd think they'd been taken in a studio – even the lightest shadow-inserts have been computerized so realistically – it's a knockout.

'The rights?'

Mikael rattles on, somehow too quickly and as if covering up, but no wonder. He's bound to be on to what a treasure-trove this CD is that he's pushed into my computer. These pictures belong to them entirely, his brother and himself. It's a deal between the two of them, reciprocal, from this one old photo-shoot. No need for a photographic agency to get mixed up in this at all. Even the invoicing can be done through Mikael's business name: the brother'll want it like that for tax reasons. All that interests me is for the rights to be ours, altogether ours, by God.

'Well, so what do you think of it then?' Mikael's cheeks are flushed a delicate pink – the man's like a shy bride. His eyes glow with a dreadful hunger for recognition.

'Quite okay.'

Mikael was clearly hoping for a little more than this, but now I have to be really on my guard. If he wakes up fully to what's fallen in our lap, he'll also wake up to the price he could ask . . . Well, one we could no doubt afford, but there's no point if we can get away with less.

'I presume you *can* use them?' Mikael's voice has a tone of actual distress in it now, and I realize it's time for the *coup de grâce*. I lay my hand on his shoulder, with a weighty, manly purposefulness.

'Of course we can use them. As one alternative anyway.' A glimmer of hope dawns in Mikael's eyes, a hope not just centred on pictures or money.

'What occurred to me as well is – it's a topical theme. All the papers are stuffed with these stories about wild animals in the towns, and . . . well, it's as if the publicity was already made: people's fears, all this talk that's going on, and . . .'

Poor chap, I think. No need to go on selling it any more. It's sold itself already.

'Come on, let's go and have a coffee and talk about money.' My hand on his shoulder's ushering Mikael out of the room, and he almost wobbles trying to walk away without making it leave his shoulder quicker than necessary.

Angel

I'm sitting in the pub, and I'm having a beer, and my heart's still thumping with happiness and excitement.

You did it, Pessi, you did it, I whisper quietly. *I undressed you, I dressed you, together we're a perfect team.*

An excerpt from the journal of Yrjö Luukkonen, frontiersman from the village of Suomussalmi near the Russian and Lapp borders, 1981

Fri. 10.7.1981: At 18.20 I arrived at the cabin and put a gummed tape on the roof against the mosquitoes. The ravens were at the carcass. The cuckoos were cuckooing near the cabin; I took some photos. The ravens finish feeding at about 21.00 hours and thereafter the neighbourhood is dead quiet. At 22.50 the sun so low the tops of the trees along the shore of the tarn turn reddish in the light. At 23.00 I see a troll coming to feed. A large male. It approaches the carcass slowly, stops from time to time to listen. The troll keeps in the shade of the trees, so that I have difficulty getting it in the viewfinder. It advances with extremely fast strides straight at the carcass, tears off some ribmeat and puts it right into its mouth. There is so little light I take no photos. Then the troll begins tearing off a bigger piece of the carcass, making very careful use of its foreclaws. I then decide to try a photo. The first click of the shutter stiffens the beast, and a second starts it upright. It disappears with its lump of meat into the forest, so quickly I can only catch a few dim shots. I stay awake until four in the morning, but the troll does not return.

Sat. 11.7.1981: During the night I look at the carcass several times to see if there is anything – there is not. I have been hoping to get my lens on a troll female with her young. No one has yet taken a picture like that. But yesterday's male sighting has been my only prize.

Sun. 12.7.1981: Still nothing. I readily understand that the sharp-eared male scared off by the sound of my shutter will not return, but I thought some other troll might stray this way.

Mon. 13.7.1981: I draw a blank. Just two cuckoos near the cabin, and at 21.00 hours three ravens came to feed. They flew off Hartikkalampi way at 21.45.

Tues. 14.7.1981: I arrive at the cabin at 19.30. At first there is altogether too much light for trolls, but a bear is soon at the carcass. Above the bear's left eye there is a hairless patch about 4 centimetres square, and that spot is swollen, almost closing the eye. White tissue showing on the edge of the eye, on the right cheek the slash of a claw. The bear feeds and departs at about 20.20. At 23.00 comes bear 2. Perhaps the trolls dare not come to the carcass now the bears have found it.

Angel

But when I get home, drunk with happiness, the door's ajar and Pessi's gone.

Palomita

My bag's weighed down with joy and clinking with defiance. I've bought some more catfood, a different brand this time. I want to know how the troll's getting on. And Mikael. I got the money back on bottles and collected little coins and bought the tin on a different receipt so that Pentti –

A scratching noise on the stairs.

A black flicker, a patch of night hurtles into the shadow behind the banister, and I know what it is.

I've seen it before. It's somehow managed to escape from his flat.

I put my bag down and quickly pull the ring on the catfood tin, push my finger into the light brown paste and crouch, beckoning with my hand in the air. I hiss a soft invitation. The animal smells the food straight away. Its ears prick up from the shadow of the banister, then it comes closer, sidling up, ready to bounce off, its tail's trembling, but finally it crouches in front of me, nostrils twitching in its little slender face. It stretches its muzzle out uncertainly, then licks my finger, as if it remembered – perhaps it does remember – the moment when it was sick and weak and I was its *mamà*.

And footsteps, footsteps! From above. I look up. The troll starts and gets as tense as a bow and arrow but doesn't fly off. Mikael.

'Thank God, thank God, thank God!' he keeps saying. 'Oh heavens. Hell. Thank you.'

He comes and takes the animal in his arms as devotedly as a child. It doesn't resist but grips his shirt with its paws like a baby ape. Mikael says nothing more but goes back up the steps, running, taking them two at a time, and I follow, because I can't do anything else. The bag and open catfood tin are left on the stairs. I don't care.

Angel

Palomita follows me through the door. I close it, go into the sitting-room and put Pessi on the floor.

I'm at a loss whether to get the rolled-up newspaper or give him as many quails' eggs as he could ever want.

'How the hell did he do it?' I ask aloud, and I don't care whether she understands or not. I've gone cold, yet sweat's flowing from every pore. Supposing that old gossip, that nosy old cow of a caretaker, had seen Pessi on the stairs?

I sit down heavily on the sofa. Palomita sits next to me. I start rattling away in a hurried, almost hysterical English.

'I beg you, let me hope you won't mention, ever, won't tell about this darling pet, not to anyone? Maybe animals aren't even allowed in this house – I'll lose him if anyone gets to know. He's no trouble. He's terribly intelligent, he always obeys me, but he wouldn't necessarily obey others. Something might happen.'

She keeps nodding, smiling in a way that makes her narrow face with its big eyes almost beautiful. This is the second time she's saved Pessi for me. I ought somehow to be able to thank her, but I don't know how. She looks at me like a cocker spaniel.

There comes a rattle from the hall.

I leap up, and both Palomita and I see the same thing: Pessi has stretched up as tall as he possibly can, the middle of his body looks weirdly elongated like a cat that's trying to grope for something high up, and, concentrating hard, with his long-nailed fingers, he's turning the knob on the doorlock.

Click.

The door opens.

Pessi looks at us with a perky curl in his tail. His whole being speaks pride.

Pride. Joy that he can imitate me, who always opens the door like that, before I go out there into the world that doesn't belong to him.

'He's opened it himself,' Palomita breathes.

In one leap I'm in the hall, and Pessi backs off from me. I shut the door, dig the keys from my pocket, turn one in the keyhole, and click: double-locked.

Then I start laughing, laughing and laughing quite irrepressibly. At first Palomita's puzzled, but then she begins shyly tittering, and I slap my thighs, hooting. Pessi's ears tremble with amazement.

Martes

When I see the layout I know this is it. This is the Tops, the year's Gold Standard, the EPICA, or whatever. It's just fab. The image left nothing else to think about but the title – and bloody bang-on that had to be, too. That's it now. In tiny typography – and nothing but the title. For *nothing* can be allowed to detract from the force of that image.

Against a pale neutral background there's the troll. It's snarling and furious – God knows what Michelangelo had to do with Photoshop to get its eyes blazing like that. In the pictures it looks monstrously tall, two metres at least, and, in spite of that, it's got a slender and whiplike suppleness and its muzzle isn't protruding, as in those rare troll pictures I've seen. No, it's confusingly like a human face. Its mane is wavy. Its coal-black coat shines. The long hooked claws on its forelimbs and back legs are sort of clutching the air. And it's in the middle of a wild skip-and-a-hop routine that's something between ballet and breakdancing. The crackling energy in the image makes you tense your every muscle instinctively, poised to jump back. And this punk-god of the animal world has Stalkers on its legs, which look as if they were made to measure.

Above the picture, in an extremely modest, almost whispering font, is the title: STALKER, THE MARK OF THE BEAST.

Palomita

When Pentti dresses me in the split trousers and wants to stuff me with two penises at once, I bite my lips and moan as I've been taught to and think about *him*.

When Pentti decides the food I've made has too much white pepper in and throws it in my face, when Pentti counts the shopping money again and again to prove I've pinched fifty cents, when Pentti takes all my clothes off for the whole day just because I've spilt some tea on the blouse he's bought me, I think of *him*. It's as if I'm hitting back, and I've no feeling of remorse.

I think of when I was helping him with his pet. When I left the open catfood tin and shopping bag on the stairs, and when I came back, the lady with the quilted jacket and the big dangling earrings was staring at them. Why had I left catfood on the stairs? Had I got a cat? And I told a lie and said I'd found a lost cat in the yard and given it food, and the woman was rude and angry. In this house no one brings in all the world's stray animals. And she snatched my tin and took it away.

But I get into no bad mood because of what the lady says, no; for then, too, I think about Mikael, who has been laughing his relief and his pride out with me in the hall. When he stopped laughing I knew I had to go, and suddenly there was a strange, empty, disappointed feeling in my stomach. But when I was almost outside the door, stealing away from the one place where even if just for a moment I feel some warmth, he suddenly held out his arms to me, pulled me to his breast and squeezed me until I nearly burst. 'Thank you, thank you, again, Palomita,' he said. Then he let me go and looked at me embarrassed, as if he was amazed himself. He tried to say something, 'I'm so happy . . . you do understand, don't you . . .', but in my dizzy joy I just touched his lips with my fingers as a sign that he should be silent, and I ran away from the joy that was flowing over me.

For no one can be so grateful just because someone has brought back a runaway pet . . . and so I'm waiting. And I'm thinking.

Angel

Pessi's sitting in my lap, sleek and black and warm. The root of his tail stirs a little against my lower belly. I stroke Pessi's arm, which has a small, firm bicep, I raise the book I'm holding higher and continue reading. Pessi's pointed ears tremble as he follows the rhythm of my voice.

I glance through the window. Outside there's a soft snowfall, dense enough to make vision nil. White death, I think.

I continue reading aloud:

Illusia never ever forgot this evening. The previous day she had lost her wings and realized that from now on she had to live on the earth. Life here for her was no longer like a picture book for children, which you look at and then throw away. She knew she had to live this book, and now she had a feeling that there was something fearfully compelling in the book, that the tints of its pictures glowed on even in the night, when the dusk of the north came down to flatten them out.

I swallow. Pessi looks in my face as if wondering why I've stopped reading, why the words have dried up in my throat. He stretches up and sees a drop of sweat on my upper lip, his little rough tongue brushes the corner of my mouth, and an inarticulate sob flashes to my throat. And outside it's snowing, snowing endlessly.

Ecke

Outside it's snowing, snowing endlessly.
  And I've left sixteen messages on Angel's answerphone.

Angel

'Pessi,' I whisper, and I stretch my hand out and slide it around his sweet, narrow, smooth, burning-hot waist. Pessi's ears tremble. I have a massive erection, as if part of my stomach and thighs were rock-hard aching flesh.

I've locked him in here. I've tried to capture part of the forest, and now the forest has captured me.

Ecke

Mikael, be at home.

You've been as slippery as a ferret, O thou golden-haired Adjutant of Heaven's Commander-in-Chief. You do definitely check your incoming calls, glance at your mobile's screen and see the number there, my number, which you don't want to answer.

You haven't come to see my source books, though I've learned off by heart everything I could amuse an archangel with. Did you know that, as Mikael, you hold the Bookkeeper's office on high: you note down all our debits and credits in the *Book of Life*. And on Judgement Day you'll initiate the Resurrection of the Dead with your trumpet call, you'll take military command of your angel host, and you'll overpower Satan and his henchmen in the last decisive battle. In the Book of Daniel you struggle against the Dragon. In the Western world you're usually garbed as a knight, and you carry a sword and a long partisan.

The spring sleet's piling up in sheets on my head and shoulders and clouding my glasses, and I want you to pierce me with your burning sword, Mikael, and, bloody jejune though this will sound, I'm longing for your glowing partisan.

Angel

Thank heaven, the doorbell rings.

The piercing buzz clears my head like a bolt of cold lightning, and Pessi jumps at the sudden sound and flashes under the sofa.

I open the door a little way, blessing the comer and simultaneously cursing myself. A peephole for the door, why in hell haven't I got myself a peephole?

'Angel,' Ecke says, almost with a sob, and melting sleet's running down his shoulders and hair.

Ecke

While I'm trying to drop some casual and breezy word about the Gustaf Eurén book, and returning it, Angel's already out on the stairway.

He pushes the door almost shut behind him and simultaneously hugs me to him – so killingly lustful and hungry that my head rocks and my legs go weak under me. Angel's mouth is on my mouth, greedy and hard, and his tongue's wrestling with mine. He stops the kiss as if suddenly forced to pull away, gasps, and his eyes are burning with such an alarming blaze it hits me below the belt, and from solar plexus to balls I'm all fire, with an incredible lava flow of success.

'Let's go to your place,' Angel says, shoving his hand in the doorway, grabbing his coat off the hook and checking the keys in his pocket with a jingle. 'We'll grab a taxi in the square.' He carefully presses the door to and leans on it, breathing heavily and looking down at me under his brows, as if I were his prey. And though I can't for the life of me think why we're taxiing all the way to my Kaleva suburb instead of stopping at his place, I know there are moments when there's really no point in opening your mouth.

Väino Linna, *The Unknown Soldier*, 1954

Hietanen tripped on an alder stump and flopped down. There he stayed, out like a light, too canned to get up. Vanhala made a handsome curve, his moonshine-fuelled plane engine shrieking, and yelled: 'Take to your parachute. Plane's crashing, he he hee . . . !'

'Plane's going down . . . it's all going round . . . everything's going round,' Hietanen spluttered, clutching at the grass.

Vanhala roared in his ear: 'You're in a spin . . . Jump for it . . . not going to straighten out now . . .'

But Hietanen's plane was fast out of control, turning and spinning down. No hope of a jump now: he just pressed on with his plane, first into a fog, and then blank darkness. Vanhala left him where he was, annoyed that the struggle was over too soon.

To one side, sitting around a largish boulder, were Määttä, Salo and Sihvonen. Salo was telling the tale very earnestly, with his hair in his eyes: 'Back home, in our parish, fires burn over buried-treasure pits . . .'

Sihvonen turned his head aside and flicked with his hand as if fending off mosquitoes: 'Come on, come off it . . . You're lying . . .'

'Oh yes, they do burn all right. The old 'uns have seen 'em. And, like this, they've got crossed swords over 'em.'

'Oh, come off it . . . These old wives' tales, Lapland witches' tales. All sorts of shit you hear. About the Russkis, for instance, they say that when they run out of men, they catch a troll, put a uniform on the beast and send it off to the western front. Watch out when you see one of those crashing through the forest at you . . . there you have it, one of the wonders of the north.'

'But who *is* from the north, then?' Määttä said. 'I'm from far enough up north myself, and I know of folks who keep a troll as a domestic animal.'

Määttä had had very little to say the whole time, and the powerful moonshine didn't seem to have got to him all that much. But now he looked at the stone and said: 'So what do you say? There it is, the stone. Why don't we lift it?'

Martes

'Now it's sold.'

'*It's sold?!*' I watch a smile slowly spreading across his face like a wash of watercolour.

'Want to see the layout?' Not waiting for a reply, I go into my office, with Mikael the Pageboy trailing after me, ready to lick up any drops of honey I might deign to drip.

I pull a print out of the pile. Mikael goes starry-eyed when he looks at the stylistic purity, economy and sheer cool pull – explosive madness, too – of our joint work, and I'd swear his eyes have gone moist as he looks up at me again.

'So stylish,' I say. 'It creaks with chic.'

'It does.'

'You can invoice us.'

'What did the client say?'

'A hit, right at the core of our fragmented postmodern age.'

Mikael gives a snort of laughter. 'No, he didn't.'

'He did, that he did.'

Mikael can't take his eyes off the layout, the black mane, the nails clawing the air, the snarling expression, the breakdance–ballet-leap frozen into a still.

'It's beautiful,' he sighs, and his ecstasy wounds me: it's an invisible slash – like a cut from a page of a book. I don't happen to have mentioned to the client that the image and the conception have come from a sub-contractor. And no point in enlightening him so that he could go to the sub-contractor direct and get for a few thousand euros a picture we're asking fifty-odd thousand for. And so the honour's mine, the layout's mine, and Mikael's got no right to look at it so lovingly.

Hey, I'm here, too, I'm just about to snap, but then Mikael's already taking his hand off the print and putting it down carefully on the table, and his smile's like extra light flooding into the room.

'I'll send Helvi an invoice for the amount we discussed.'

'What about a beer now? Isn't this the moment?' I ask, before I even notice I've said it, and I bite my lip – hell, I'm not getting into all that any more. But Mikael's stand-offishness is a challenge: it's as if he didn't see, didn't hear, damn it, that I'm here – me, me, Martes – Martes, whose company used to be so sought after. Why isn't he hanging back, looking for any reason to stay? Why's he not chatting aimlessly just so he doesn't have to step outside the door?

'Oh. It would have been . . .' Mikael's sigh is genuine and gentle. 'But, dammit, I've gone and booked myself up for this evening.'

'Surely you can spare a few minutes?' I get a grip on myself. 'Or, well, yes, in fact I've got all sorts of stuff on myself.'

'Another time.'

'Yep.'

I stand watching him go, and, I don't know why, somewhere inside me there smoulders a slight smudge of disappointment, smoulders and spits a thin grey smoke.

Palomita

Strange things are happening in the peephole.

Pentti has stopped there, talking with the staircase woman. The woman keeps nodding and waving her hands about. She puts her face up to Pentti's ear and says something with a serious look. Then she draws back, folds her arms and shakes her head.

Pentti takes his wallet from his inside pocket and gives her a visiting card. He seems to be stressing something, and the woman nods as if she means it. Then Pentti fishes a banknote out of his wallet. He squeezes it into her palm with two hands.

I hardly have time to take the stool away and get into the kitchen before Pentti's here in the flat. His face glows bright red as he shouts out what on earth have I been doing. He says he knows everything now. I've rung neighbours' doorbells. I've tried to bring stray cats into the building. I've brought shame on Pentti in everyone's eyes.

He hits me twice, and then he's had enough. He says that if I like catfood that much perhaps I'd like to eat nothing else all next week.

He doesn't say where he's learned all this. But I know now.

Angel

I've been having a shower in Ecke's matchbox of a bathroom, where
you have to wriggle down on to the lavatory seat with the wash-basin
pressing on your lap. The shower curtain's nurturing a rank and multi-
farious ecosystem.

I slide down next to Ecke under a grey military blanket. Ecke has
taken his glasses back from the bedside table and is reading something.
I pull the cover my way for a moment. Aleksis Kivi's classic novel, *Seven
Brothers*.

'You're not serious!'

'Yes, yes. You're in here, too.'

'Ah ha! No doubt I'm Jussi of Jukola, the hemp-haired mope.'

'No, a much more angelic figure. Remember the wan maiden?'

'Huh huh.'

Ecke ignores my scornful snort and begins declaiming in the style of
some juvenile youth-club performer:

Once upon a time there dwelt in a certain mountain cavern a dreadful
troll, the terror and scourge of mankind. He had the art of changing his
form into anything he wished; and around the neighbourhood he was
seen abroad, sometimes walking as a handsome youth, sometimes as a
beautiful maiden, depending on whether he thirsted for man's or
woman's blood.

'What is this, some hint about transvestism?'

'Stop it. This is cordon-bleu tripe.' He skips a few pages and then
lowers his voice meaningfully, dramatizing his tale by leaning my way
and half whispering. Then he straightens up and booms, making my
eardrums tingle, and I groan, pressing my hands on my ears, only half-
joking. And that, too, tickles him.

And there the hapless maiden was, shrieking, struggling and pulling
away in her agony, but in vain. With a wicked howl the troll dragged her
into the depths of his cavern and decided he would keep her for ever

beside him in the dark bowels of the earth. For long, long years the wan maiden stands on the mountainside every night, in storm, rain and biting frost, beseeching forgiveness for her sins, and no complaint is ever heard from her lips. Thus she spends the gloomy night, but with the dawn the merciless troll drags her back into his caverns.

I feel vaguely disturbed but not because of Ecke. When he's being sincere, free from the barricades of affectation, the Café Bongo smoke and the compulsion to pull, Ecke is in fact boyishly attractive – yet fucking intelligent with it: the starry-eyed innocent and yet, hell, how streetwise, how titillatingly cynical. Rather like the mousy chick you get in American films who, once the Commemoration Ball comes around, leaves her glasses and tooth brace on the bedside table and bowls over all the guys who've been giving her the brush-off.

'What about this then?'

Ecke flicks over some more pages, strikes his breast theatrically and then flourishes broad arcs in the air with his arm.

Looking at her lovingly, the young man took her in his arms, kissed her, and soon the wan maiden felt a delicate stream of blood sweetly cascading through her drained veins, her cheeks flushed like a cloud at sunrise, and her clear brow gleamed with joy. But now the raging troll, bristling with fury, crept up the hill to drag the maiden back again into his dungeons –

I snatch the book from Ecke with fond determination – this is obviously what he's been working up to the whole time – thrust him down into the mattress and listen to him letting out little whimperings as I pinch his susceptible spots. And I think about the troll.

Ecke

O heavenly being.

In the swish of his wings, in the glow of his halo I sink into the mattress. And I let out a cry.

I've never been so happy in my life.

And I've never in my life been so crushingly sure that the one who's holding me so voluptuously is thinking of someone else.

What flashes before my eyes is the catch of the month I met in the pub – that patently self-deceiving, laurel-crowned latent. And when Angel draws me towards him, groaning, I try with all my power to be Martti, I'll be for him whoever he wants me to be.

Angel

Pessi keeps growling, letting out little strangled throaty sounds, as he dances an angry little ballet around me, his tail horizontal and stiff.

His nostrils widen and twitch. I try to touch him, but he bounces back like a sprung spring.

'Pessi.' My voice is coaxing and soothing, even a little apologetic. What on earth's the matter with him? I've been away as long as this before, haven't I?

His nostrils: his nostrils are twitching, his ears are flattened against his skull. The smell.

Ecke's smell is on me.

The smell of a strange male.

Still steaming from the shower, I sit down on the sofa, smelling of pine soap, and my heart spreads a sweet warmth throughout my whole being when Pessi finally comes over to me and pushes his dark muzzle against my shoulder.

Martes

Three pints of Guinness are making the roots of my hair tickle, but I have to go back from the pub to switch off the machines. Here we are again, one of those afternoon-pint sessions that stretch until the end of office hours. But who cares, if there are no meetings for a change, no deadlines about to be missed?

Viivian and I drew lots for which of us would leave the pub, crawl up to our offices, switch off the computers, and make sure the burglar alarm's on. Now everything's okay, and I'm wondering, shall I go back to the pub, where Viivian may still be sitting, sipping her perry, when I see a CD on the table. It's Mikael's CD-Rom, the one with the Stalker campaign pictures on, and I shove it into my shoulder bag. It has to be returned, of course.

Ancient Poems of the Finnish People, **VII. 3. 1237, 1933, Suistamo**

Brothers three be we,
Three brother boys we be;
One went after elk,
The other for a hare,
The third bid fair
To snare a troll.
Back there came one brother,
Hare's paw in his palm;
Back there came another,
Fur of fox was on his arm.
Back there never came the other.

Martes

I ring the doorbell, and Michelangelo opens the door, wearing his bathrobe.

He's so astonished to see me, he doesn't budge, doesn't let me in – just stands swaying in the doorway, keeping the door half-closed, as if I were some door-to-door salesman.

I dig my cover out of my shoulder bag, the CD, and brandish it between my thumb and forefinger.

'Just popped along to give you this back.'

Mikael's expression shows he's used to getting his stuff back by post. 'Ah! Thanks.'

He's just about to close the door on me, with a strange look on his face – evasive, anxious – mumbling something about my putting myself out unnecessarily . . . could have picked it up at the office any time himself. I see him glancing back out of the corner of his eye, again and again.

'Got visitors, have you?'

'No, no . . . no one.'

'Just beginning to be afraid I was bursting in on something . . . some social gathering.' My eye wanders over Angel's bathrobe.

'No, no.'

'Er . . . mind if I use your loo?' I'd been expecting a look of delight. I'd been expecting to be lured in. I'd geared myself up to be a bit formal and then perhaps agree to a coffee or bottle of beer, just passing the time of day. But this is something quite new to me. I'm supposed to be the evasive one, I'm the one who sets the pace and decides what happens and, above all, what doesn't happen.

Mikael's glancing back into the flat again, as if listening – maybe he's got something boiling on the stove. I take advantage of his preoccupation to push the door open and step inside, gently but purposefully.

Mikael jumps. I don't know what's on his mind, what he imagines my intentions are, and his eyes have no trace of that moist adoration I've become accustomed to and even enjoy in small doses, like an exotic but slightly outlandish spice. Mikael's eyes are darting left and right, he's mumbling, muttering . . . it doesn't suit now, another time, he's just on the way out, in a terrible hurry.

He'd push me out of the door if it hadn't already formed a wooden wall between me and the stairwell – with me as a wall of flesh between him and the door.

It's infuriating.

A stifling miasma of Mikael's aftershave is lingering in the air, the whole flat reeks of some aroma which, at that strength, is the whiff of lust itself and jerks me humiliatingly into a half-erection.

And Mikael grabs my arm – hangs on me as if I were the rail of a storm-tossed ocean liner.

'It's no go now. I really mean it.'

'Two seconds in the loo, and then I'm off – not bothering you any more.' I try to sound like a martyr, but Mikael's rejection of me is like being stabbed with an icicle.

He stations himself in front of me, and I try to worm around him playfully, and we perform a ridiculous minuet: we dance the two-step. And then he gets hold of me, starts shoving me towards the door, and I flare up. The stout seethes in my head, and, more violently than intended or actually needed, I grab hold of Mikael's shoulders and thump him against the wall.

'Get going now, Martes,' he says quietly. 'For Christ's sake, just go.'

And then.

In a falling shaft of light.

Nightmare.

Part 4

Darkness Takes My Soul Away

Laurentius Petri, Rector of Tammela, 'An Extract from His Sermon at the Ecclesiastical Assembly in Turku Cathedral', 1666

The ancient Finns have also named the Evil Angels: Demons/ Gnomes/Forest Sprites; the Sons of Kaleva/Timesprites/Blackmen/ Hillmen/Trolls/Werewolves/Ogres/Goblins/Watersprites/Mermaids . . .

Martes

It stands on two legs. It's a snarling demon.

It's a sci-fi movie monster.

This steep-angled spotlight's sharpening its bony body, its long claws, its nervously twitching limbs. It walks with a spooky softness, sways closer to me, raises its forelimbs – it's raising them threateningly high. Into the attack.

Its claws are aimed at me.

Its grotesque face splits in a hideous snarl as it lets out a hissing growl from its throat.

I feel the hot urine flowing down my thighs.

'No!' I hear Mikael shout.

And the monster's going for me.

Angel

No. Not this.
  Anything, but not this.

Martes

An umbrella's leaning against Mikael's wall – it's been in reach all the time – a pure reflex makes me grab it and wield it across the front of me. But I'm dead slow compared to this ghoulish beast. Its fearful scalpels are flashing at my eyes, faster than light – the umbrella's just enough to fend off everything but a ferocious slash I feel on my cheek and temple. My vision narrows to a spotted fluorescent yellow. It glows for a second, and everything around me sways sickeningly.

Somewhere, terrifyingly deep inside me, something wakes – a reflex.

Quicker than thought, in a single coordinating storm of my synapses, they all fuse: my endless karate sessions, the frustrated youth seeking his manhood – kung fu, Bruce Lee, a teenage mutant *ninja* – and I squeeze my eyes tight shut, swing around in a crouch, and the umbrella chops the air like a samurai sword.

It hits something that makes me expect a twang like a taut bow, but instead I hear a high squawk – a screech like the cry of some large bird unknown to science. I open my eyes.

Something warm, sticky and dark is streaming down my neck on to my shoulder. I fly off the handle, and Mikael's hall turns into a thin funnel, bright yet clouded with a snowstorm, and I see on the floor somewhere at the end of the tube a bloodstained black umbrella, its spokes mangled on one side, and I can make out, somewhere under the hanging coats, the monster – it's shot off there to hide – a motionless monster after my blow, a horned, black, sharply defined, toothed-and-nailed statue. And Angel's on his knees before it, spitting out words.

'Get the hell out of here, Martes. Do you hear me? Go to hell, and get there *fast!*' No trace of warning in his voice, no concern for my escape or me – just pure hatred.

I put my hand on my cheek and my temple, and I realize the skin's ripped open on both my face and my scalp. The blood's flowing, it's forming puddles on the floor, and the front of my jeans are wet with cold piss. And in all this surrealistic show Mikael's staring at me, half kneeling under the coats, hugging a devil.

Liisa-Marja Iivo, *The Satan Sects of the Tornionjoki River Valley and Kittilä in the 1910s*

The classification of the troll as an animal species in 1907 was an undeniable sensation in biological circles. It was indeed a rare event – though by no means unique – for so large a mammal to be revealed to science in this century. Reported sightings of the *Felipithecus trollius* were, of course, relatively abundant, especially in the north, where the so-called 'white nights' facilitated animal sightings; but these reports were not considered reliable in scientific circles, certainly not probative. Several finds of animal hair, bone splinters and claws were considered hoaxes, and serious study of these finds was not even set in motion.

Though the troll does indeed prefer inaccessible areas, hibernates and buries its droppings, thus leaving no observable traces on the terrain, it is nevertheless anomalous for no single troll carcass to have been found in the wilds until 1907. This anomaly has clearly given impetus to a belief that has made its appearance in more recent folklore: that the trolls bury their dead.

The troll's demonic attributes naturally left their mark on the zoological discovery of the species. The incontrovertibly prodigious scientific importance of the discovery was almost paralleled in historical impact by the collapse of the mythological paradigm, whereby a centuries-old folk tradition was set in quite a new light. Consequently, it is not beyond comprehension that there were also reverberations outside scientific circles. What causes some surprise, however, is the magnitude of the reaction in certain contexts, the most notorious being the formation of the Satan Sects of the Tornionjoki River Valley and the town of Kittilä.

It is of the greatest theological interest that the same event – in this case a widely publicized discovery in the biological field – caused the manifestation of almost diametrically opposed socio-religious phenomena in districts so close geographically.

The movement in the Tornionjoki River Valley congregated around Eerikki Nesselius (born: Niemi), who ministered in Ylitornio but originally came from Pello (1879). Nesselius was a novice preacher whose religious orientation was firmly rooted in the Laestadian religious movement. Nevertheless, he was by no means a prominent figure in the public life of the area until he became acquainted with the newspaper reports about the discovery of a troll carcass. Post-haste, Nesselius journeyed to Helsinki and demanded to study the conserved troll, but he obtained access to no more than the photographs available. According to the diaries that survived his decease, Nesselius was particularly impressed by the troll's tufted tail.

He returned to Ylitornio and without delay began his proclamation that the Devil had returned to the surface of the earth. He produced an amalgam of the recent troll discovery with the so-called *Earth sprite Sermons* that Lars Levi Laestadius preached in the 1840s and 1850s, in which Laestadius attempted to persuade the Lapps to renounce their demonic beliefs (cf. e.g. Nilla Outakoski: *The Image of the Earth Sprite in the Sermons of Lars Levi Laestadius*, Scripta Historica XVII, Publication of the Oulu Historical Society, 1991). The following extract from Nesselius' book of homilies, *The Living Satan* (Kemijärvi, 1911), condenses his views:

> So all here can picture for themselves how every single sin performed is as a seed that falls on the ground, which, sucking black power from the earth, grows in might and flourishes, until it blossoms forth as a full-grown living Satan. A true and living forest demon has been delivered into our midst to remind us of our misdeeds and warn us never to sow further sins as long as we live. The Lord God Almighty has placed a living Satan among us, and why? Because its task is, when thy evil has ripened, to manifest itself as an incarnation of that evil, to bring a vision of Hell from the wilderness, to figure each sin thou hast performed on the way.
>
> Because our race of men is stiff-necked, and has rejected the Lord's commandments, the Lord God has raised these fearful sons of Lucifer from the ground as a warning of dread to us all. Thou, meditator of guile in thy heart, take care and look behind thee on the pathway. For is it not already there, flitting behind thee? The figure of a living Satan, sent to torment thee, which at God's command has loomed from the earth and waits only for his best occasion to snatch the wrongdoer in his fearful claws. Thus are we all placed on dreadful trial . . .

Nesselius was soon attended by a few hundred followers. Especially great weight was given to his words by one Hirvas-Uula, a well-known reindeer-herdsman, who did not personally ally himself to the sect but did come when invited to confirm his sighting of trolls to the congregations. Nesselius in all probability rewarded the herdsman for this with money or drink, as the witness's statements inevitably stamped him as a miserable sinner himself: he had seen 'the forest demon', according to his own testimony, half-a-dozen times, while hunting hares, for example, though, for the most part, very far off, it is true. In one of the most striking of his tales he described seeing as many as four trolls, working together to drive a wild reindeer on to stony ground to break its leg.

On the basis of the photographs he had seen and the drawings he made from them, Nesselius fashioned a wooden carving, representing a troll, which at the present time is preserved in Ylitornio church (though not for public view). The carving went with him on his preaching tours, and during exalted prayer sessions his assistant set it peering through a door left slightly ajar or from a window and, when it had been observed, snatched it briskly away. This may have powerfully increased the congregation's sense of sin and Nesselius' impact.

The statue fraud was disclosed in 1911, and thereafter the congregation soon faded away; but still in the year of his death Nesselius swore that the 'Satan' peering from the doors and windows was genuine. The statue, therefore, was allegedly a genuine troll, which this time the Lord Almighty, to demonstrate his might, had transformed into wood and not into the conventionally expected stone.

According to Nesselius, then, the troll's origin was divine, though it did represent evil. This was actually the only clear factor the Kittilä Satan Sect had in common with Nesselius and his sect.

The Kittilä Satan Sect was not particularly well organized, nor did it have a leading figure such as Nesselius. When news of the troll findings arrived in the Kittilä neighbourhood there was an eager revival of the local lore about trolls and earth sprites. Individuals were found who had had dealings with trolls, according to their own accounts or those of their relatives. Those who had had a personal encounter with earth sprites included the Old Lady of Koskama, Aapo Jänkkälä, Antti Vasara and Reeta Helju, who had found behind a fence in Tepasto, in the parish of Ritalaakso, an actual earth sprite's house. In the village of Sirkka, in the parish of Kittilä, the Mäkelä family had entertained a troll child as a changeling, and in Palo a householder had knowingly fraternized with a demon; and so forth.

The revival of the stories and their dramatic heightening briskly developed into a village cult in Kittilä. Along with this went an increase in social status, depending on the ability to demonstrate that a forefather, or even the individual himself, had had dealings with trolls. The knowledge of the trolls' factual existence decisively changed tales and legends into supposedly valid histories, and the people associated with the stories became warlocks or 'the tribe of the Devil', revered and feared as semi-witches.

The Church became concerned about the Kittilä Satan Sect only when it began seriously to resemble a religious sect. Some of those who regarded themselves as belonging to the tribe of the Devil began to shun the church and churchgoing, for one of the most commonly believed myths about the trolls was that they had fled further into the wilderness in order to avoid the Christian faith and, specifically, the sound of church-bells. The landmarks that the stories specified as troll dwelling-places began to become the sites of sacrificial gifts, like those typical of the ancient Lapp stone-idol culture. The people who belonged to the tribe of the Devil began to act as the community's unofficial leaders, whose advice was sought on both public and personal questions. In the Kittilä cult, trolls were thus regarded as a species of forest gods that the human race had, in its mindlessness, driven into the deep forest; but the trolls could, as it were, transfer on to a person they met some part of their supernatural aura. An essential and characteristic viewpoint in the Kittilä stories is that the accounts repeatedly report a human resourcefulness that prevents the troll from harming the person encountered. The members of the tribe of the Devil were thus doubly exalted: they had received the right to have contact with the nature gods; and they had emerged from that contact alive.

Eerikki Nesselius heard of the cult of the tribe of the Devil, too, and he did attempt a short mission in Kittilä. Success in general remained poor, but this much effect Nesselius did have: the Kittilä folk were long tormented by their reputation as devil-worshippers. It is worth mentioning that precisely this reputation unquestionably led to a short 'normal' outbreak of something resembling Satanism in the district as late as the 1980s. Still today there are evident remnants of the thinking of the tribe of the Devil in the Kittilä neighbourhood and elsewhere in Lapland, especially among the older age-groups.

Angel

After that attack and the blow he received I thought Pessi would be a quivering mess, but no, he's gone quite stiff – stiff as a wooden doll. Doesn't even seem to be breathing. And when I hug Pessi – when I cradle him in my arms, rock him, drawing long, sobbing breaths – and see through the lianas of the sleeves and trench-coats blood pouring from the reeling Martes' scalp and cheek, dripping through his fingers on to the floor. I also see that, for Martes now, our relationship, mine and his, mine and Pessi's, is crystal clear.

Martes

A troll. A real live troll! I've been a complete dupe.

There they are, incarnate: the Tops, the year's Gold Standard, the EPICA or whatever. In Mikael's hall off Pyynikki Square.

The Tops, the year's Gold Standard, the EPICA will all drift away like smoke if this goes public. Get this on to the *Evening News* placards the day after tomorrow and the Stalker campaign's kaput. I want my campaign.

I feel cold, though my heart's still pounding a hundred to the minute.

As the door bangs to behind me I'll bet Angel doesn't even spare me a look. He's pushed his face so hard up against that monstrosity's black mane – breathing it in, breathing in that horrible stiff black tar doll.

Dr Spiderman

When the telephone rings in the middle of the night, I have to observe, with a sigh, that I've almost been expecting it.

Angel

Spiderman stares at Pessi in the hall, hands deep in his trench-coat pockets.

He gives a faint laugh, and it makes me want to clout him. Pessi looks quite dead, half curled up on the spot where he was driven by that bloody Martes going berserk with the umbrella.

Spider touches him, presses his large canine head against Pessi's back for a moment, listens.

'What do you call him?' Spider's voice is quiet and almost tender, but somewhere behind it you hear a demonic glee, annoyingly out of key with the situation. 'Robin, the Boy Wonder?'

'Pessi.'

Spider cackles hysterically, cawing for a moment.

'Make us some coffee. And then we'll have a little chat.'

Dr Spiderman

His troll's like a shred of night torn from the landscape and smuggled inside. It's a sliver of tempestuous darkness, a black angel, a nature spirit.

Can you tame darkness?

Perhaps you can, if, to start off, it's very, very young, helpless enough, in bad enough shape . . .

One of night's small cubs.

Angel

'There's something at the back of my mind,' Spider ponders. 'A certain theory I once came across.'

Here in the kitchen, steam's curling up from our coffee mugs, Spider's thoughtfully munching on the liver-pâté sandwich I've made him, while my knee's jerking up and down under the table: do something, do something, do something, dear Spiderman.

'According to this theory, it might simply be a defence mechanism. Somewhat similar to the opossum's resort to faking dead. In situations of extreme threat, the troll doesn't try to escape but goes into a catatonic condition, its body temperature going down and the whole organism's activity slowing. Puts itself into cold storage. Bound to be a moderately effective factor in the survival of the species and not unique. On a pitch-dark night, completely motionless . . . extremely difficult to observe, and the lowered body temperature could also hinder detection of its scent or . . .'

I put my coffee mug on the table, grasp it again – can't take a swig, not one. Pessi's curled up in a corner of the hall, like a shining black masterpiece stolen from some morbid sculpture park and hidden away among the winter coats, the leather jackets and the skirts of smelly rubber capes.

'Will he come out of it?'

'How the hell should I know? The theory's pure hypothesis, entirely based on serendipitous sightings and sheer hearsay. There are simply no systematic studies about these creatures. But, anyway, it would explain one thing –'

'In the tales the trolls can turn to stone in the light of day.'

Spider looks at me bemused, and then a smirk of amusement spreads across his face.

'Very good. Playing possum would at least account for how those tales arose . . . But that's not what I meant. Imagine the forest, imagine the untouched wilderness, where a troll's on the run and feeling threatened, hunted. It makes no distinction between being hunted or studied: what it hears is the high-pitched whirr of a small plane or a helicopter's clatter. An enemy's coming from the air and, when the adrenaline peaks above a certain point, snap, the troll freezes into immobility, looking like a tree trunk, cool as night.'

'Yes, but what next?' I take a look into the hall. Pessi's a striped shadow, one among the rest. You have to look hard to make him out amidst the hanging coats.

'Short of that, there's no evidence, nothing measurable, it's all sheer speculation. Because nothing's been recorded with thermographs. Or with any other human device – never, really. Think about that one.'

Dr Spiderman

There's the rustle of a jacket in the hall. The troll's moved. Angel lifts his downcast, bloodshot, red-rimmed eyes from the table: new hope's burning in them.

'I'd better be off, in case he gets upset again,' I say. I recover my jacket from the chair back, put it on and try to walk with the greatest possible discretion into the hallway, prudently avoiding any sudden movement, as when a large menacing-looking dog is brought into reception.

'I have to warn you . . .' I say, keeping my voice low, while hearing on the parquet the brief, light scratch of a claw coming out of torpor.

'Oh, I'll be safe with him. He's terribly intelligent, he's altogether tame –' Angel snaps, but I interrupt him, wearily raising my hand.

'That I don't doubt, but all this is completely illegal. Are you aware that, according to Finnish law, you're committing a hunting offence?'

'A hunting offence?'

'A rare one, but there are precedents. Last year, near Kuhmo, two men trapped a bear just as it was coming out of hibernation, and for months they maintained it in a couple of square metres of cage. They used it for training hunting dogs.'

I see Angel blush. 'There's nothing at all like that going on here –'

'And if you succeed in keeping this injured friend of yours hush-hush, all well and good. But I should tell you, if anyone gets wind of my having had anything to do with this, I'll be struck off.'

Angel nods, hardly even looking at me – his ears and eyes are fixed so rigidly on the waking troll that I feel a stab of irritation; no, outright jealousy – and that brings my mind around to the other thing.

'And for your information, too,' I say, and my tone does wake Angel up for a moment, so icy-chilly my voice is, 'I've no way of verifying this precisely and scientifically, but the whole joint reeks of pheromones.'

'Pheromones?'

'Yes. The special scent molecules animals send out into the atmosphere. They signal rutting or fear or the state of health, or the status in the troop. They manipulate and control and tempt other members of the troop and the species. And your troll's emitting some very powerful pheromones.'

I rub my eyes. I'm so tired, so hellishly tired.

'Those pheromones could be used to make a fortune. A colossal fortune. Luckily no one realizes it. Not even you.'

Angel stares at me. The words reach his eardrums but no further. His face is registering a defiance I recognize: a ten-year-old boy setting himself up against an adult's authority, jaw jutting, mouth straightened to a line, ears deaf to all argument.

My imagination takes off: rows of troll-pens somewhere in the north – in Ostrobothnia, say – those supple black flashes of forest lightning now fettered behind chicken wire, and the most unpleasant ways possible found for milking every single homoerotic molecule from their glands. And I close the door behind me and fill my lungs with a deep draught of that stairwell smell of damp stone and dead coffee.

Angel

When I wake my first thought is: Pessi! I hear a scratching at my side and turn my head, and Pessi's sitting – or, rather, sitting's the wrong word; he's knotted up in a modern dance posture with all his limbs sticking out in various gravity-defying aerial directions, and he's licking one of his paws, trembling with exuberance. He seems breezy, contented, enveloped in an atmosphere resembling an inaudible echo, wafting up from a deep, gratified purring.

Pessi's little red tongue is pushing tightly and sensuously between his fingers, in a single-minded, moist, red-and-black, back-and-forwards movement. I drag him towards me, almost with a wrench, breaking all the promises I've made myself, drawing in a deep asthmatic breath of air – and then let go of him immediately, dive out of bed and, hand trembling, legs trembling, dial Ecke's number. And when a sleepy voice answers, I ask, 'Can I come around immediately?'

In the hall, for a moment, I don't believe what I see.

Easy to believe I'm in the nightmarish continuation of some twisted erotic dream.

About a metre above the floor, on the white textile wallpaper, there's . . . a painting.

There are evident lines, and even something you could, with good-will, call the outline of a figure. And once more, somewhere at the back of my cranium, a little warning bell tinkles.

Finnish prehistoric relics.

A rock painting.

Yesterday, agitated and exhausted, I neglected to clean up.

The wall painting has been painted with Martes' blood.

Martes

The iodine has turned my skin orange and it still stings enough to make my eyes smart. The scratches are raised at the edges. An awful lot of foreign micro-organisms can be transferred to the victim through animal bites and scratches. So said the nurse at the accident ward, who told me to settle matters between myself and the owner of this rampaging dog.

I shall do, but in my own way. And in my own time. When it'll be most advantageous.

On my cheek there are four parallel reddening streaks. My temple's had to have a patch of hair shaved off, and in my own grotesque way I find this punkish slash hellishly cool. Eight stitches have been punctured into it.

Angel

Two days I kept Pessi hidden and locked away in my large attic store-room. He was so distressed and ears-laid-back that I had to bring him back in.

If Martes had wanted to do something, he'd have done it by now.

I've made Pessi a present of pastel crayons. Obviously they smell wrong: he doesn't even pick them up in his paws.

How intelligent is he, really?

Why, when he's had blood at his command all those times, hasn't he decorated the bathroom tiles with victory signs – guinea-pig and gerbil figures, painted in violently primitivistic strokes?

Perhaps the slaughter and consumption of a little rodent is not such a big deal, not the sort to sing songs about or inspire the painting of frescoes. But the defence of one's territory, the wounding of a great enemy, that is. Is it?

Or was it a painting, after all? Was it perhaps nothing but fortuitous pawmarks and smudges my guilty and hysterical mind fused into a configuration?

The hall's fibreglass-treated wallpaper is now clean and shining.

Why didn't I take a Polaroid?

I place two mugs upside down and quickly switch them about, and Pessi doesn't point out which has the titbit underneath but looks at me swiftly, as if weighing the situation up. And then, quick as a flash, he pushes over both mugs, grabs the pat of catfood in his claws and dashes off to the window-sill to eat it, relishing it like a child with ice cream . . . And I wonder which of us is the fool.

Palomita

Sun. I immediately thought how wonderful it is when it's warm. Warm at last. I opened the window, but outside it's colder than ever.

How stupid it is to wait.

How stupid it is to think.

> *I confess to Almighty God*
> *and to you my brothers and sisters*
> *that I have sinned through my own fault*
> *in my thoughts, and in my words,*
> *in what I have done*
> *and in what I have failed to do.*

I beat my breast for each sin, as I've been taught at Mass, I beat until my hand hurts and my chest hurts, but it brings no relief.

> *I ask blessed Mary, ever virgin,*
> *all the angels and . . .*

I beat, beat, beat, the more because I let my thoughts break off. No, not the angels. From them I ask nothing. At least not from the sun's own angel, the one who chased Satan from heaven.

I beat my breast once more, so I start to cough, and quietly I try to sing the *Salve Regina*, which I only remember a bit of.

> *To you do we cry, your banished children of Eve,*
> *to you do we send up our sighs,*
> *mourning and weeping*
> *in this vale of tears . . .*

I cry to Mary. Not to you who in the last days will weigh our souls. Not to you, angel of the Last Judgement.

Angel

And again I close the door, again I escape.
Escape from myself, escape from Pessi.
If only I knew what I was escaping from, what I'm afraid of.

Ecke

Even though he avoids me sometimes.
Even though he's always rushing off.
These things I don't think about.
In spite of everything, this is the nearest thing to heaven: Angel's practically living with me.

'Trolls and Gunmen Play Hide and Seek at Pulesjärvi', *Finnish Morning Post* (29 March 2000)

In a mystery incident yesterday at Lake Pulesjärvi near the Lehtisaari campsite two men received gunshot wounds. Surprised by a wild beast, they were struck by the off-target bullets of an unknown gunman, presumed to be attempting to defend them.

These local Pulesjärvi men had long suspected the Lehtisaari campsite buildings were being used as a squat during the winter closure. Inspecting the cabins, they did find several traces of breaking and entering. They also found primitive bedding made of moss and spruce branches.

The dwellings had also attracted animals, for when they opened one cabin door a large troll came running out at them. One of the men tried to aim a shotgun at the threatening animal, but then two shots were fired from the forest nearby. One shot struck him in the shoulder, the other grazed his companion's shin. The still unidentified gunman, whose target was presumably the troll, was likely to have been wielding a high-calibre hunting weapon or military rifle.

According to wildlife researcher Erik S. Nyholm, it is not uncommon for a famished predator, a lynx for example, to seek shelter in a hay barn or empty storage building, especially when looking for a place to hibernate.

Owing to the premature spring, the gunman's tracks have not been detectable in the almost snowless forest. The police are investigating the affair.

Dr Spiderman

I lean on the window-sill, pressing my forehead against the coolness of the glass. I'm some sort of tragic figure in a second-rate movie, gripping his ice-tinkling whisky glass and staring into the murky dark, silently whispering *Angel* to himself. More inaccessible than ever, just now he's as far beyond my reach as if he were sitting on the moon.

My eyes drag the dim street, and suddenly my thoughts and memories seem to be merging into a double exposure out there: a black shadow.

An almost invisible flickering black shadow – two black shadows, absolutely soundless, economically fluent as flowing water; two pieces of darkness are dissolving in the dusk around the streetside refuse bins.

And I can't be at all sure: did I really see what I think I saw?

Angel

When I get back home, it looks as though Pessi's decided to empty his litter-tray on to the hall floor. I'm getting to know the kinds of tricks he gets up to. I've put locks on the cupboards, even the fridge, and I did think I was getting on top of his dexterity.

But fuck it. Now the doormat's covered with newspaper shreds, so fine they're almost down to a cellulose dust, and then I realize the paper's been torn up and chewed, not cut up with scissors, as in Pessi's litter box.

Pessi's out of sight, and when I go further into the flat, I realize something terrible's happened. I see a swelling on the bed from something under the bedclothes: Pessi's gone into hiding – hiding because of something I know nothing about.

I go over to the bed and gingerly touch the bulge. It starts and kicks and gives a sob, and then subsides again, trembling. I realize Pessi's terribly upset about something.

I'm stumped. I go back into the hall and start mechanically scooping up the mess of paper – in my hands: I'm not going to risk blocking up the vacuum cleaner with all this stuff. Then my hand comes on a more substantial piece of paper – the glue's kept it in one piece. It's an address label. An address label with the name MIKAEL HARTIKAINEN on, my address, and several rows of code. A magazine's arrived.

It's the same mag I have in my shoulder bag – one I'm inordinately proud of and therefore bought at a kiosk as soon as I saw it. The back cover shows an advertisement, the one I know I'll yet grab a few prizes for, the picture I've been paid seven thousand euros for.

The best of the pictures. The dark bestial dancer, the paws – no, his hands – stretched out towards the photographer with an expression half-rage, half-love, and on his legs the eye-catching Stalkers.

He's seen it.

He knows what it is.

He can read pictures.

And he hates them.

Or this one at any rate.

Yrjö Kokko, *Pessi and Illusia*, 1944

But Pessi scarcely took in that he had only started learning to know himself when he saw his image in the smooth surface of a gloomy, deep pool.

Ecke

There it is in the mag, Angel's pride and joy.

It's fine, a hell of a fine picture. Extremely artistically done. Part of Angel's and that fucking Martti's collaborative world, which I shall never have access to.

At the same time, something's beginning to nag at my memory: I'm associating the picture with something – something embarrassingly erotic, no, more than that, pornographic, but I can't recall what. In any case, Angel's hit the jackpot, the picture's a sensation, a hit, shamelessly sexual yet without being sexual.

Then it begins to dawn on me.

I go into the sitting-room to the cartoon shelf.

I'm positive I've got it around, somewhere here. It's a fantastic rarity, a pirated edition, and probably no more than about a hundred copies of that issued. Found it in Copenhagen, from under the counter – the sort of shop where they don't usually hide away even the raunchiest stuff.

I turn it up at the back of the shelf, tucked out of sight behind several large illustrated books. The draughtsman certainly didn't have the use of any decent photographs, let alone live models. Comparing the pictures with the Stalker advertisement, I see lots of differences: even though the ad troll seems huge, it's younger than the creatures in the drawings. They're swaggering, full-grown, exaggeratedly muscular, exaggeratedly human-looking beasts, endowed with, considered biologically, outrageous genitals, but then that was the rule with this guy. Page after page, I see how the cartoonist has thrust all inhibition aside and invented frightful, bestial erotica, where the other partners are slim, blond, pouting boys, joyously submitting themselves to all sorts of abuses.

I turn back to the cover: poorish paper, tepid colours, but the text in large, proud letters: *TOM OF FINLAND, TROLLS AND FAIRIES*.

Dr Spiderman

'Definition always presupposes its opposite,' I say to the woman in the camouflaged combat suit. She's trying to get me to converse, though what I most long for is just to blunt my faculties here in the Café Bongo buzz and stop myself feeling any more pain. 'Define the word "normal", and you have to define "abnormal". Define "humanity", then you have to define what humanity *is not*.'

'Isn't that just the same impasse?' she asks.

'Not in my opinion,' I reply. 'If you suddenly had to say what's abnormal, you'd certainly list far fewer things than there are – you'd automatically leave them outside the normal, without listing them.'

The woman's clearly lost the thread, but she's dogged. 'So, okay, provided you're defining humanity. Or intelligence. Is a dolphin intelligent? Is an ape? If the criterion's use of language, then those two, at least, fulfil it.'

'Bees have a language, and yet I shouldn't go so far as to call them particularly bright. And in addition they also create elaborate building complexes – so there's another of the criteria proposed: manipulation of the environment. That, too, they fulfil, but even so I wouldn't let bees jump the queue to get into Oxford.'

'Of course you wouldn't, because it's more convenient for them to make honey for people. And therefore they have to be what they are, what we've defined them as – human property – and humankind is of course Lord of creation.'

'As for that, I have to stress that the Judaeo-Christian ethic has never had any special force for me as a guiding principle,' I say dryly. 'What other religious organization has ever led mankind further from our affinity with nature? As soon as the god of Israel took over the reins, animals were no longer permitted to serve as gods, and all other ritualistic connections between the species, including sex, were excised.'

The woman's getting fretful, feeling side-tracked. 'No, that's not what I mean. Just this, that we won't recognize the chimpanzee as a person until it rises up against us in rebellion.'

Palomita

Ang hiya lalaki, nasa noo. The men wear their honour on their foreheads. *Ang hiya ng babae, tinatapakan*. Women's honour is trampled on the ground.

I knew it couldn't be true. It was too good to be that.

Weeks have gone by, and still he doesn't come. He doesn't remember me, and I can't, I can't and I don't want to go through his door any more, not after that hug, which means he's the one who must make the next move.

Sometimes I ask myself why I don't go, why I don't take some catfood again or some home-made cake, but that's how it's always been and that's how it always will be.

We're those who don't know their own good; we're those who have to know our own place, or the world'll fall apart.

We're watered-down people.

Men have no sex. Only women have.

And I can't rise up against Pentti. It's impossible. It's forbidden. A woman doesn't abandon.

But what can I do to him, if *he* abandons *me*? If he's left with no alternative?

And I think about *him*.

Something inside of me whispers, you only think about *him* because he's not Pentti. He's a door that opened on to a blank wall.

Martes

When our new client, this hockey-team, brought in their brief, they didn't know what a jackpot they were hitting.

I bring up the best picture on to the screen, a splendid snarl, the most overflowing with contempt for the camera. I isolate the head and paste it into my own Photoshop data file.

Then I clarify the tone and use a couple of filters, solarize it, then cancel that, clear away the pixel dust, draw in a fine line here, another one there, deepen the colour of the lines to a hundred-per-cent black.

My scalp stings. My teeth clamp together.

Looking back at me is the troll's face – wild as hell, the bloodthirsty snout tuned to a few lurid lines, tuned until it sings.

'Viivian, come and take a look at this.'

Viivian, Viivian the Assistant, Viivian the Dutiful comes. Viivian whistles.

'Well, now, that's wicked.'

'Compare it with their first.'

Together we look at the old logo of this ice-hockey team that's become a client of ours. A tailed creature's fumbling with the hockey skates on its legs. Looks like some illustration in a crappy animal story for children.

'This'll be the best in the fucking league.'

'No question. That lion of HIFK's a sick kitten beside this.'

'Fuse it with the name logo, Viivian. Cut it on to the old font and then try a couple of new ones, something more robust – you can work out something yourself.'

'Above, below or around?'

'Might go better around.' With my finger I outline on the screen some curved lines above and below the roaring beast's head. 'The Tampere . . . Trolls.'

'What a bunch of fucking fashion freaks.' Viivian's sigh is genuine.

'You said it.'

Ecke

I play the mincing parlourmaid, and Angel laughs out loud. It's a real belly laugh, he's not just humouring me. I serve him his coffee mug with a bow, leaning to kiss his forehead, which has a few locks of hair glued to it.

'Is there a paper?' he yawns.

'A moment, Your Highness . . . Honoured sir.'

I bring in the *Morning Post* from the hall floor. It smells of printer's ink and the damp spring. Angel rakes his hair with his fingers, forming a golden halo, and I love him to bits, until it hurts.

He's hardly opened the paper when he gives a violent start. The coffee mug crashes on to the floor in three pieces, the brown liquid seeps along the cracks in the floorboards.

'Bloody hell, no!' he hisses.

Angel

He looks at me from the garish advertisement. It's him.

With a low-browed grimace of a grin, a seventeen-year-old ice-hockey prodigy, garish in red-and-green sports shirt, is glowing with out-and-out fearless puberty – and just about brain enough to read a Superman comic: slightly acned skin, an attempt at a macho moustache struggling for life under his nose. Actually he might be fanciable if his shirt didn't have *that* on it.

The thing's a news item: the new logo design has been praised to the heavens by the team's management.

It's sewn on the shirt front. It's black and white, graphically reduced, a facial shot in the midst of a chaos of spruce-green, blood-red and sponsors' logos.

It's him. Or if not himself some unidentified being painfully like him.

Like my Pessi.

Ecke

'I've got to be off right now.'

Hastily I try to fish for some information, but nothing doing. So his brother's photos have been used without permission? I can see that it's annoyed him, but why does he have to dash off, and where to, and why right now?

'Home.' Angel's already pulling his jacket on, his mouth's tightened into a slit like a knife-wound. He's a bundle of nerves and ice-cold and won't allow me to touch him.

Slam.

The door bangs to much harder then necessary. The echo on the stairway's the thud of an executioner's axe.

I stand like a zombie in the middle of the room. It's as if some unspoken taken-for-granted deal had suddenly been broken by one of the parties, with no consultation on my part whatsoever.

I flop on the bed and draw in a wheezing breath of air. There's something shiny under a chair. The chair Angel hung his clothes on overnight. I bend down and look more closely.

His keys.

The keys of Angel's flat.

Out in the hall I've already rung Angel's mobile and listened to the engaged signal for half a second when it dawns on me: what a chance this is to perform a knockout service, a truly super-duper parlourmaid stunt. A chance to seduce those bloody blue eyes into that fucking rare but all the sweeter look, when he realizes, just for a second, that I actually exist.

Martes

'You fucking ape.'

It takes a moment before it dawns on me who's on the other end. It's Mikael, the sweet, understanding Michelangelo, exuder of tender breaths and Calvin Klein odours, who's now brandishing a burning sword. He's on his mobile: the traffic's roaring in the background.

'Fucking shithead. By what right?'

'Every right in the world, my darling Mikael.' I feel such icy contempt for him I can allow myself a phrase I'd never otherwise mouth. 'The full rights, here with me, in black and white.'

'Full rights for the Stalker campaign!' His voice is getting high-pitched, and it gives me the creeps to think I've ever been in the same room as this fancy-pants.

'Teach yourself to read what you're putting your name to. What we have, on paper, are the full rights, for this office's use.'

'Thief.'

'Has your nature-photographer brother been kicking up a row? That Russophile who manages to photograph extremely rare wild animals in what appear to be studio conditions.'

I wait a quarter of a second before I give the *coup de grâce.*

'Or, more precisely, your late brother.'

Angel

On the phone, I'm running in and out of the Sammonkatu Street traffic, threading through shopping-laden ladies on the pavement, panicking, gasping for breath. To wait for a bus or a taxi seems unthinkable. I'm imagining: Pessi's on the sofa asleep – against the white cover he's a bottomless black hole into outer space. And the newspaper's on the hall floor, a pale patch of threat in the dim light, the paper where there's . . .

But I'm brought up short as Martes' reference to my brother thumps into my consciousness. He pauses a moment, and then his voice has gone back to his previous purring and controlled baritone.

'You said the original photographer was your brother. It so happens that he's been dead for two years. That I established straight away . . . as soon as complications set in. Do you want to tangle with the law now? Do you want me to stand up in court and say who took the photos and when and where?'

My voice is a mere whisper when I can find it: 'And so now you think you can play the whore with those pictures any way you want.'

'I don't think, I know.'

And his words throw me back again to Pyynikki Square and my gnawing worry. But what is it I'm afraid of? Am I supposing Pessi's going to wake up and take the morning paper in his prehensile little paws and start leafing through it, thinking, in his little round head: Gosh, look what's happening in the world again. Haven't they settled things with Indonesia *yet*? And then see the news item and explode into another fit of hideous aggression?

That's exactly what I *am* afraid of. That I'm letting him down once more.

'I'll ring your client.' I'm at a dead end, so I can't do anything but reel off empty threats.

Martes' fucking equanimity begins to waver a mite.

'You'll not bloody well sabotage a campaign we've planned and sold and in part been paid for! The hockey team's whole public set-up, from their sports gear to their writing paper and the car stickers – can't you fucking well grasp it? This isn't some teeny-weeny small-time contract, you know.'

'Do you ever think about anything but money?'

'Do you ever think about anything but that one thing? I've never taken it in before – the link between bestiality and paedophilia.'

I suddenly go bright red. It's as if Martes had landed me one, right in the teeth, with his knuckles.

'It's nothing of that sort, you filthy-minded shit. Your mind's such a poisoned sink, you . . .'

Martes interrupts me.

'Start fighting me about this, and I'll screw the balls off you. Because I know what you are.'

Martes

My stomach's a foaming churn of red rage. If Mikael rings the client and starts kicking up a fuss, bang goes this fee. Our good name will be ruined as far as this client goes. Goodbye to the Tops, the year's Gold Standard, the EPICA.

I'm taken aback when he gives a short laugh, quite soft and quite brief.

'What am I, Martes?' he asks, and though he's still panting he sounds calm and a little sad. 'What am I? And what's our relationship?' His voice is surprisingly untroubled.

'We've had no *relationship*,' I say, and my heart starts thumping harder, and I hate it. 'Never.'

His manner's something I haven't been able to gear myself up for. His rage, his aggression, I can deal with. I can mouth off sharp put-downs, like anyone else in the communications business, but this sad little melancholic laugh floors me.

'Except for our working relationship,' Mikael says.

'And that ends here, if I've anything to do with it.'

'Do you remember that time, after eight pints, by the Tammerkoski railings?'

'For God's sake, don't try to drag me in on your own sick fantasies!' I yell into the phone, and naturally just then Viivian walks past the room's open door. I kick it shut, and my voice is a whiplash, hissing between my teeth, 'Damn it. I want to make this thing clear once and for all, now –'

'No need to. To me it's plain as daylight already.'

He draws in a breath I can hear. I also hear his voice changing as he moves into some echoing precinct.

'I'll come back to the question of the rights on those pictures. I have to put a stop to this now.'

Click. The hang-up warning goes. The sound rises higher and higher until it's screaming in my ear, so piercing my eyes are about to pop out of their sockets. My cheeks are glowing, and I listen to it, listen to it, until I grasp that it's telling me what I have to do.

I have to put a stop to this now.

Part 5

While the Other Loves the Night

Lars Levi Laestadius, 'Communion Sermon', 1849

Therefore they are black as Tartars when they come again to rend with their claws the dwellers on the face of the earth, who carry crosses on their breasts. But these creatures of the Underworld are like the forest demons, who howl like wolves when they smell the scent of blood, and some laugh like harlots when the Devil leads them astray.

Palomita

A noise. Footsteps on the stairs. I freeze.

Hope. Stabbing pain.

They're coming up the stairs.

Mikael!

I fly to the door, get up on the stool and glue my face to the door.

My disappointment's sickening: it's some young man I don't know, dark, wearing glasses. He's on his way to Mikael's but doesn't know Mikael's not at home.

Not yet at home, but he'll be home soon.

He's never stayed away for long.

Today I waited so long on the stairs with my shopping bag that the stair-case woman came out and saw me, pretending it was by chance. She saw some strawberry wine and chocolate on top of my bag and started being sugary and nosy. I could hardly breathe, and I whispered to her as if she were my friend that I was expecting a visitor today. A wonderful, important friend.

I saw her eyes flashing.

Angel

As soon as I'm through the outside door I start digging in my pocket for the keys. I try again. I stop and try all my pockets.

They're not there.

I have to get to Pessi. I have to get to him right away.

I've never in my life bothered that caretaker woman about anything, but now I rush up to the first floor like a panicking hare and ring her doorbell, trembling: be at home, be at home, be at home.

Palomita

More steps – hurried – and now it's him, now he's filling up the peephole's little round world.

Before I can get down from my stool I see he's not going further up but ringing the hair-curler woman's bell. He rings and rings – he's all nerves – and then the door opens, and I see his knees are almost giving way under him as the woman stands in the doorway smoking a cigarette. Mikael's explaining something. He leans on the door-post with one hand, tapping nervously while he speaks. The woman disappears inside and then she's back in a moment, holding a bunch of keys, which she gives to Mikael, stressing something, smiling knowingly, and Mikael keeps nodding as if his head might come off.

I hop off the stool – now, now, now, just now – and open the door, and Mikael's had no time to take even two quick steps towards the top floor when I've invited him in and said I've got something very, very, very important to say, and Mikael stops and wrinkles his brows but then he comes over and says 'Well?', and I take him by the arm and pull him inside.

And I know the staircase woman has seen it all.

Ecke

Angel can't have got hold of another key, because his doorbell rings faintly for the fourth time behind his door. Maybe he's not even managed to get home yet or even checked his keys. All the more delightful for the keys to be already waiting here and, on top of that, an excellent bonus. I make up my mind to go in: I'll be all set when I hear the footsteps. I'll fling the door open and shout 'Surprise!' to a bemused and overjoyed Angel.

Besides, it's high time. For some mysterious reason he's never invited me into his home. He'll not fly insanely off the handle – will he? – if I turn up inside without being asked? Intruding into the abode of the angels?

And of course, now I remember: there's something else. Gustaf Eurén and *The Wild Beasts of Finland, Illustrated in Colour*. I've a hell of a good reason for going in and getting the book. Angel hasn't returned it, though I've asked him for it several times.

It's a fucking valuable book.

I pull Angel's keys out of my pocket and weigh them in my hand.

I have the right. Don't I?

Palomita

He looks worried and a little far away, but he's here after all – his golden hair, his eyes – the only ones that can turn a blind eye to my breasts, my black hair.

He asks what's upsetting me. I look him in the eye and smile: he's got to read from my face how much I like him. Because this is the last moment to let him see. Because there's no going back now.

And just as I'd thought, just at the right moment, it happens, what had to happen, the solution.

The key turns in the lock.

Ecke

The key turns in the lock.

Angel

I turn and, bloody hell, there's Koistinen, Palomita's very own commercial traveller.

Koistinen's shortish, pot-bellyish, reddish and baldish, a little bit of everything but nothing right. The creeks on his temples are glistening with a few sweat-drops.

'So this is what's going on.'

His voice is quite calm and rather insolent. As if he'd been expecting something like this all along and now his suppositions have been confirmed.

'A whore is a whore.' He gives Palomita a shove, making her stagger against the wall, and she lets out a swift flood of speech, a mixture of English, Finnish and some language I don't know.

'Cut it out, slut. Let this Casanova do the explaining.'

I try to salvage the remnants of my dignity. 'Mikael Hartikainen, from the floor above, good morning.' I offer my hand, but Koistinen evidently sees it as a leg of boiled fowl fresh from three weeks in the fridge.

'Just turn your back here, it seems, and the shagging starts.'

'Half a mo, there's some complete misunderstanding. I left my keys somewhere – I was just over there, getting the master key, when your wife wanted to ask me something. And since we know each other slightly from before –'

Koistinen's face shows me that this is the last straw.

'From before is right. But I've laid it on the line to her: no dealings with strangers.'

'Dealings? There've been no . . . dealings here. A couple of times we've said hello on the stairs and thus become acquainted and –'

I was about to say 'paid a call', but I realize straight away how this pink Neanderthal would read it.

'So how *acquainted* did you become?'

Koistinen's proceeding like some Finnish film: he's the country parson booming questions at some milkmaid suspected of intercourse with a farm hand. And the whole situation's so bizarre I'd be bursting into hysterical laughter had I not spotted in Palomita's eyes the glow of a feeling – fear, and something else, something unidentified and daunting.

Just then I hear, directly from above, a noise – seems like something heavy falling – a piece of furniture or something. It's from the floor above. From my flat.

Pessi's doing something he shouldn't.

I've got to get back up there, stop this farce as quickly as possible. Koistinen's jaw is jutting out like a bulldog's. He's decided to turn the hall into a courtroom and thrash things out with delectable long-windedness. He's the chief justice. He's the jury. In my hurry, I decide to be the surprise key witness.

I spread my arms, jut out my hip, shrug my shoulders, sweep my hair back and purse my lips, camping up a nasal whine:

'Goodness me,' I crow. 'There can have been *no hanky-panky* here! Koistinen, haven't you realized: I'm . . . hmm! Good grief!' I swing my hips. 'Well, one of *those!*'

Koistinen gives me a short look and, to put the cherry on my performance, I give him a wink.

His fist flashes out like lightning, bashes me on the cheekbone, and the other thumps into my belly. He's cursing and blinding, and I fall through the open door on to the stairway, flat on my buttocks. The door slams shut behind me. When I get up I hear a faint shriek, which suddenly breaks off.

Ecke

Light's seeping into the hall from deeper in the flat. My God, the first thing I set eye on, through the sitting-room door, is the end of a white-leather sofa. Everything in sight cries out style. Glass and chrome, natural wood, white, grey and black. Lithographs on the wall.

I'm floored. I'm altogether too vulgar, altogether too tasteless for a hotshot with a home like this. I'm an animal.

Shoes at least I must take off.

When I bend down to slip them off, I realize the flat's permeated with a strong spicy forest smell, the same heady smell that sometimes wafts around Angel. Angel's aftershave? I instinctively sniff my body. Oh, bloody hell, my man-made fibre college shirt's been on for a week already, and it tells.

I put my shoes neatly side by side under the hooks, peek in the hall mirror, pull my comb out of my hip pocket and try to get some sort of order into my mop of uncut hair.

I hear signs of life on the stairs – but they're coming from lower down – it's not Angel yet.

I go into the sitting-room, the kingdom of light tones, the wonderland of careful consideration. Straight into an interior-design magazine.

Just then behind me on the left there's a scratching.

Something black darts against the white.

And then everything goes red.

Angel

My cheek's hurting as I climb up the stairs. There won't be much more than a bruise there, though, and that can be covered up with makeup.

I've been gripping the master key all the time. It's sweaty and hot. I open the door, and I smell something.

Metallic it is, and pungent – mixed with a smell of fresh excrement.

I go through the hall into the living-room. And then – I want to throw up. But I can't. Every muscle's totally paralysed.

Ecke.

Ecke. Near his hand, on the floor, there's my bunch of keys.

Ecke's laid out on the floor, and just about everything's covered in blood. The white leather sofa's a lurid death cap toadstool, spattered with red. Another large – and oh how red – mouth has opened in Ecke's throat. Ecke's bowels have emptied themselves into his jeans.

When I *am* able to throw up it's some sort of relief.

I crouch down, vomiting on the parquet.

Ecke, Ecke, Ecke – oh, Ecke, what have you done?

Why did you come here – you, so clever, so sharp-tongued, more than a little blasé and yet the bashfully laughing little boy, slightly at sea in life.

So inventive in bed, ready for anything, frisky as a fish.

You, whose sweat-and-sperm male smell has sometimes flickered around me – and wafted to those black, sensitive nostrils, as a blow, a threat, a signal from a foreign troop.

Pessi's bouncing about restlessly but a little stiffly, as if his legs were on springs. He looks at the body and me, over and over again. He's proud as hell but at the same time slightly worried. He doesn't know what he should do, eat or give the prey over to me – to me, the only troop he's got left now.

Dr Spiderman

They stand in my reception, dark blue, slightly uncomfortable, exuding their authority.

'And the situation requires us to have a veterinary surgeon at hand to supervise any anaesthetization.'

'A large predator? In someone's home?' I ask, raising my eyebrows to convey the greatest possible surprise, playing for time, though as yet I've not the faintest idea what to use the time for, and my heart's pounding. O Angel, how art thou fallen from heaven, son of the morning!

'Neither did we, sir, at first take the report altogether seriously. But after seeing several extremely compelling photographs, and certain bodily injuries, we found that the allegation was worth looking into. It seems, on the face of it, very unlikely – a wild animal of this calibre harboured in a block of flats. But to ensure security and fulfil the legal requirements, we require a veterinary surgeon on the premises. If anything untoward happens, then the animal can be –'

They maintain a half-second's pause, and I know precisely what's in question.

'Put down.'

'Yes.'

'If it's not . . . put down, then what happens to it?'

The police look at each other; this question they hadn't anticipated.

'Be sent for biological research, I presume. It's such a rare animal.'

My consulting hours are ending, the evening light's gilding the window. Angel.

The policeman fidgets nervously.

'Presumably, sir, you have all that's necessary here on the premises . . . we heard from your receptionist you'd performed such duties before.'

Put down sick dogs, yes. Big dogs, too.

'I'll be ready immediately. Just a couple of minutes, please.'

The policeman nods.

'May I ask you to wait over in the waiting-room for a moment?' – and relief flows through me when they turn with a nod, exiting just as I'd hoped. Luckily doctors – even animal doctors – are obeyed instinctively, without question. Even the police don't stop to wonder why, just now, they have to wait outside.

I lift the receiver and my hands are sweating. While the ringing tone buzzes and buzzes and buzzes, I rehearse stammering sentences in my mind: go, go, go at once, take Pessi somewhere far away, go before they get to you . . . And the phone buzzes and buzzes and finally – as an immense surge of relief floods over me – Angel finally replies.

Angel

Mobile at ear, I stare at Ecke's body.

'Actually,' I say equably to Dr Spiderman, 'I've already been thinking it might be time to go.'

Dr Spiderman

And so I, Jori Hämäläinen, doctor of veterinary surgery soon to be struck off, walk towards the police car, where Special Branch officers are waiting.

Angel

Blood's roaring in my ears, and some wordless, defiant march is ringing through my head, keeping time to my panic and banging away as hollowly, heavily and fatefully as my heartbeats, when I switch off my mobile and chuck it down the lavatory. I put on my forest-green Gore-tex, the light and durable waterproof outfit I bought for Lapland when I spent a week there with Pauli but haven't worn since. I lace up my thick-soled, waterproof, ankle-supporting trekking boots, the ones I bought to impress Jens and wore them in well enough doing it.

Could be I'll have to cope in the forest a long time, but time's short. I throw together a small rucksack, a Swiss army knife, water dashed from the tap into an empty Evian bottle, a plastic cigarette lighter, a woollen sweater and a spare pair of socks. Nothing much in the fridge except some vacuum-packed reduced-fat salami. Can't take a lot of clothes, but the spring's been amazingly warm, about twenty degrees centigrade since mid-April. Pessi's bouncing about impatiently. He smells my cold bitter sweat, my fear and panic.

It's night but not dark – blast the April light! I grab a blanket off the sofa, wrap it around Pessi and lift him up in my arms. Oh, how bird-boned my little troll still is, how light and slender – grown a lot but still much the same as six months ago, when my life was changed and I let a changeling into my home.

Palomita

The bruise on my cheek's burning, through pressing it against the door, trying to catch just a glimpse of Mikael in the peephole. He goes leaping down the stairs, two at a time, wearing funny clothes and clasping a long round bundle. He's running so fast I'd have no time to open the door and shout, so that Pentti's double-locking the door doesn't seem as bad as it might.

Then the police come, just a couple of minutes after Mikael's gone. I'm sure now that Pentti's done what he said he'd do – he's called the police to take me away. In Finland, he said, women who deceive their husbands are sent to prison. I'll be there all my life long, and my family'll have to pay back all the money Pentti's spent on me, and my name'll be dragged through the mud. But it's not our door they're coming to, and then I realize I wished they were – that they'd get here before Pentti's back from the pub.

The police come up the stairs with a big net and a big muzzled dog whose claws scratch and slip on the stone steps, and one of them has a funny-looking long-barrelled gun. I hear Mikael's doorbell, hear someone shouting through the letterbox, and then the noises as they break the door open. For a while it's quite quiet, then one of the men comes back down with his heavy feet; he's got a sad doggy-looking face and a long yellowish jacket, not a uniform. He sits on the stairs and presses his head in his hands, and a moment later two men come up carrying a stretcher.

It makes my hands ache horribly, but I begin banging on the door and shouting, so they're bound to hear.

Aleksis Kivi, *The Seven Brothers,* 1870

Juhani: We've been harrying a bear, we have, a dangerous brute that pretty soon would be snuffing out both you and your oxen. A vicious Bruin it was we slaughtered, and thus did we a great public service for our homeland. Is that not a public service – to winkle out wild beasts, trolls and devils from the world?

Nobody pays any attention to me ⟨...⟩ in trekking gear, with large mohair bundles in their ⟨...⟩ taxis all the time. The driver's eyebrows go up, ⟨...⟩ ⟨...⟩ns. Pessi, thank God, is perfectly still in my lap, ⟨...⟩ sounds through the thin woollen fabric and sniffin⟨...⟩

The drive to Kauppi takes no more than ⟨...⟩ iver says little. Occasionally he looks at me in th⟨...⟩ ny sweaty brow. I dig a banknote out of my pocket ⟨...⟩ hand. I don't even look to see what it is, but it mu⟨...⟩ start lurching off from the roadside to the forest. I'm d⟨...⟩ before I hear the taxi irritably accelerating off. Now, if men⟨...⟩ ⟨...⟩e, we should be able, keeping the setting sun behind us, to get through the Kauppi forest and reach the outskirts of the Lake Halimasjärvi nature reserve. It's the only route for avoiding too much human habitation, and that way we'll get into the Teisko forests.

I've been on the point of falling over several times, and Pessi's annoyed. He wriggles and frets under the blanket. I decide we're far enough from the road, put him down and peel him out of the bundle. His eyes are bright with excitement, his ears trembling, and his nostrils twitch at the pungent riot of forest smells – his tail's a tensely whipping antenna, registering everything.

Just then I hear a sound, a sound too early for the time of the year, but an unmistakable sign that spring is here, and I know that Pessi can now – for ever and irreversibly – leave me. The sound's as sadly monotonous and repetitive as a funeral bell.

A cuckoo's calling.

Anni Swan, *Silky and the Trolls*, 1933

'You never get out of a troll's cave once you've drunk a mug of trolls' honey.'

Willow cried out with fear when she saw the two big hulking brutes. 'Don't be afraid,' the young troll whispered. 'Nothing bad will happen to you.' He looked at the girl pleadingly: 'Stay here. I'm the only one of the troll people who longs and yearns like human beings. When I was little, my mother exchanged me for a human child. She wanted me to grow up like a human in skill and cleverness. But my father couldn't stand people. He brought me back and put the child there in my place. But anyway, I was lying for seven days and seven nights in the human child's cradle, and I heard the human mother singing her lullabies. Since then I've only been half-troll, the other half longs to be back with people.'

Dr Spiderman

It feels really great to be drunk.

All the most agonizing and sick and stressful things feel, in a certain phase, quite – well, possibly – bearable.

You can analyse them as if through a befogged glass wall – study them without needing actually to touch them. Drunk, you can think about things as if you were observing poisonous insects inside tightly lidded jars of thick glass, while a sober view would be a walk through thickets of the same swarming creepy-crawlies likley to land on your unprotected neck or leg if you're not alert every second.

I don't think about the young man's body.

I don't think about where Angel is now.

I think about a story of forest maidens, vivid, whispering shadows who lure young men into the deep forest and snare them with their spells, so the men never return.

What was it, ultimately, that lured them there? Not the flutter of a lovely shapely arm in a wild-spruce copse, no, nor a lock of hair tossing behind a rock, but the waft of a fierce erotic charge in the air, a trail of pheromones.

Smell must be somehow connected to the cohesion of the microphyle. Could be, for instance, that a smell only affects the males: it might be the way the troop's younger members signal to the alpha male their readiness to work with him and their subordinate position. For instance, that would explain why Angel's troll didn't attack him, didn't try to kill him but, on the contrary, protected Angel's territory whenever he could. Obedience. Didn't chew through the computer wiring, didn't rip the sofa covers when he got on to them. Angel was his alpha male.

That would explain a great deal more.

A pheromone that cuts across the boundaries of species? By no means an impossibility. Musk, for example, it sets off both the arctic ox and the sultan in his harem.

A pheromone that only affects males? Axiomatic. But what about a pheromone that only affects *certain kinds* of males? Males for whom it's particularly important to have an effect on other males?

Why not?

But is there in all this – and it's a question I put to myself with a fearful relish, as if I were venturing out on to crackling new-formed ice – something altogether different from the sum of the molecular events?

Why are they here?

Why were they – and, judging from the legends and tales, very much so – associating with human beings just at the time when human habitation began in earnest to encroach on the forest lands? After that, with the onset of a new age, they shrank back into myth and legend. Even after they'd officially been discovered they went on lying low. But now there's some new upheaval occurring, similar to the one when man first began trying to push the trolls out of their own territories.

It's happening.

They're on their way back and beginning to aspire to how things were in the age the tales tell about: stories of trolls dwelling quite close to human habitation, entering into commerce with human beings, taking an interest in cultural exchange by infiltrating their own offspring into human households . . .

They're coming back, and the dustbins and tips are their new sacrificial stones.

They're coming because they have to. Large-scale forest industry, pollution and the diminution of game have cornered them.

Global warming.

I laugh out loud and go for some more drink. I'm out of whisky, so I scrunch the cap off a gin bottle, pour myself a glass, raise it and at once the Finnish forest's flooding around me.

Pessi. I almost look at the floor by me – what's he doing here – is he about to jump into my arms? And then I realize, and my cheeks go red. Gin. The smell of the forest. Juniper berry and Calvin Klein. How powerful and associative it is, man's olfactory memory!

I'm pushing the glass away, but then I tighten my cheek muscles and annul the flavour. I control a shudder, though first my mouth's full of cold and then my belly full of hot ignis fatuus.

They're on their way back and doing what the sparrows and pigeons and rats do – living alongside us, whether we like it or not. They're eating our leftovers, they're even stealing a little, and sleeping in our abandoned buildings and barns, as in the tales. They're pushing out their own territory into ours, little by little, so we'll not even notice until they're already in our midst.

I hope they'll be satisfied with that.

Samuli Paulaharju: *Reminiscences of Lapland*, 1922

But the surest and most indisputable evidence of the earth sprites'
existence is that many people of our day have seen them with their own
eyes, even spoken with them and kept company with them. And we
have to believe these people, for they are elderly Christian folk, who do
not reminisce about vanities.

Angel

All of a sudden Pessi goes rigid.

We're fairly close to the Lake Halimasjärvi district already, and nobody has disturbed us. Fortunately, the sun's rays are slanting more and more, and little by little dusk is beginning to shroud us.

I've drunk from brooks, and I've been happy to know that, whenever I want, I can fall asleep under a forest spruce, tented by branches that reach the ground and resting on a copper-coloured bed of needles.

Pessi has walked along with me, diverging into bushes certainly and at times disappearing completely – God, how quietly he moves in the forest! But, despite my fear, he hasn't vanished among the firs, taking paths of his own, where I know I could never follow him.

But now he freezes, and his tail moves in a way I've never seen until now. It slashes in a semicircle, electrically tense, expressing, I think, both excitement and slight fear and . . .

. . . great and deep love.

I've no sooner taken in Pessi's reaction than a black shadow darkens my field of vision.

It has loomed from behind a tree, like a ghost in a nightmare. It wasn't there a moment ago; now it is, and my whole body goes rigid: suddenly I'm a fast-breathing, not particularly delicious prey, a piece of meat wrapped in Gore-tex.

Pessi's going berserk with joy.

He leaps up at a huge male troll – conceivably a muscular, magnificently glossy big brother of the specimen I saw in the museum – and he's like a puppy making up to his mother: he fawns and paws and bounces and licks the male troll – his father perhaps but an alpha male all right – until the troll half casually sweeps him behind its back with its left forepaw.

And what this troll has in its right forepaw stands out cruelly clear. *Somehow I did semi-consciously guess: the guns missing from the Parola armoury and all those other strange stories . . .* So my terrified mind whispers, as the ogre raises its other hand, swings the military rifle on to its haunch and clicks off the safety-catch.

'Man Wanted for Homicide',
Finnish Morning Post (22 April 2000)

The police want 33-year-old Tampere photographer Mikael Kalervo Hartikainen for questioning on suspicion of homicide. Called out to Hartikainen's flat on Tuesday, the police found a young man's body there. While investigations are under way, the police are withholding information as to the mode of killing.

Hartikainen is known to have fled his flat after the event and taken a taxi to the suburb of Kauppi, after which his movements are unknown.

Hartikainen is five foot ten inches tall and of athletic build. His eyes are blue, his hair strikingly blond. He was wearing a green Halti trekking suit, decorated in red at the collar and cuffs. Hartikainen may be armed and, according to the police, is extremely dangerous.

Any sightings of Hartikainen should be reported directly to the police 24-hour helpline, 219 5013.

Angel

It waves the gun barrel with a movement that's idiotically well known
from the movies and yet chillingly strange when performed by –
　An animal.
　An animal?
　But the signal's clear. We're on our way now, and I'm a prisoner.

Yrjö Kokko, *Pessi and Illusia*, 1944

'Have you ever seen a human being?' Illusia asked Pessi one day.
'Once, yes, I did once see a human being,' Pessi replied.
'What was he like?' Illusia went on.
'He was very much like you and me,' Pessi said. 'But I didn't stay looking at him long.'
'Why not?' Illusia enquired.
'He was so big. I saw him over there on the heath, by a sandpit where the birds were having a bath. The heather was just coming into flower, the blue-winged butterflies were peacefully sucking its nectar, when, all at once, I was standing face to face with a human being. Then I took fright.'
'Why did you take fright?'
'He looked me straight in the eye, and fear poured out of his eyes into mine.'

Angel

The sky ahead's growing lighter. It's five a.m.

We're deep in the forest, in the midst of the kind of untouched tree-land you can't even imagine if, all your life, you've been confined to the fake woods adjoining cities – the so-called nature reserves that, in reality, are more like parks: embroidered with paths, cleared of undergrowth, illuminated, provided with benches and full of trees almost all exactly the same age. But this forest's another thing. It's gloomy and tangled, it cascades violently upwards from its mossy floor to the sky, as if the earth were thrusting it out of its breast and bursting with the effort. It's full of struggle. Species fights against species, a creeper's suffocating a tree, a twig's thrusting moss aside, for everything's in short supply: light, air, food.

In the midst of all this green-and-brown chaos we advance quickly and almost silently. Nothing but my panting breath and the crunching of my hopelessly clumsy trekking boots trouble the dawn twilight, as Pessi and the big male lead me along indistinguishable pathways. They're troll paths, imperceptible to the eye. But what seems an impenetrable-looking thicket or an unclimbable cloven rock is, on closer look, a shortcut. We go forwards as if the trees, rocks and thickets are a mist we're melting through, as quiet, capable shadows.

No human being can catch us, not on foot anyway.

Martes

A man's wanted for homicide.

Wow.

That wasn't quite what I had in mind. I did want to damage him, of course, have criminal charges brought against him – the info was pure self-defence. But now it looks as if some other party's driven the whole thing off the road.

I've no idea what's happened, but what of that? Wherever Mikael is now, or soon will be, he'll not be ringing clients or disputing rights about the pictures I've so carefully made inaccessible to others on my hard disk and my backup CD. Stalker's already commissioned outside advertising. Every Finnish city'll soon be showing on all three sides of every triangular hoarding three different pics of a lasciviously grimacing dancing troll, rampaging in a leap, dance-step or position of impossible flexibility – nursed in his tightly fitting Stalkers and looking like black lightning frozen into a still.

Uno Harva, *Ancient Beliefs of the Finns*, 1933

Like domestic animals, human beings can be lost in the forest, especially if they happen to tread on a 'forest-elf path', or a 'sprite's field'. The folk of Rukajärvi tell that a person who has walked across a 'forest sprite's tracks' will never find his way home again. In Estonia a belief has existed that when *külmking* – 'coldshoe' – who 'mostly wanders the forests' has 'been on the face of the earth', someone may step on his tracks, whereupon the person, even though his own home be in sight, will not find his way back again. The same belief has prevailed among the Finland Swedes: 'he has trespassed on the forest sprite's ground' or 'stepped on a troll track'; nor is this fancy, which has prevailed with the Russians among others, unknown in Sweden.

Many examples show that in those times, especially since such happenings could occur on your own doorstep, what was in question was not going astray in the great forest but falling into a weird condition where everything was otherwise than in our world.

Angel

In the shade of a fir tree between blocks of mossy rock, the cave looks like a narrow black mouth.

The sun has risen beyond the forest. Slanting rays are filtering misty golden streaks through the spruce twigs and dappling the moss with glowing spots.

Two shadows emerge from the rock, so imperceptibly they seem to have precipitated themselves from darkness to light. They come quite close, nostrils twitching, and their strong animal smell is like Pessi's but wilder, more pungent, muskier. And one of them reaches out with his nailed paw, making me freeze, for those daggers could rip my stomach open with a single swipe. But the paw doesn't maul me. It goes into my jacket pocket, and the prehensile, skilful, sensitive fingers seize the lilac-coloured plastic lighter.

When the troll lights it, I see it's not handling one of these for the first time.

Sunrays are beginning to flow into the cave entrance like a warm fluid. The trolls' irises narrow so much that they almost disappear completely, and the sprites turn and withdraw into the cavity. The big troll swings the barrel of his gun with the tiniest of economic gestures, and I understand.

Pessi has come to my side; his tail's trembling and twitching, and he looks up at me expectantly.

Far off somewhere a cuckoo calls.

I take his hand and step inside.